BEST-LOVED
STORIES
BY
HANS CHRISTIAN ANDERSEN

BEST-LOVED STORIES

BY
HANS CHRISTIAN ANDERSEN

Retold and introduced by Neil Philip

Illustrated by Isabelle Brent

A LITTLE, BROWN BOOK

First published by Little, Brown in 2010

Text copyright © 2010 Neil Philip
Illustrations copyright © 2010 Isabelle Brent

ISBN 978-1-4087-0284-0

Designed by Tegan J Humphryes
Produced by Omnipress, UK
Printed and bound in Dubai

Little, Brown
An imprint of
Little Brown Book Group
100 Victoria Embankment
London EC4Y ODY

www.littlebrown.co.uk

An Hachette UK Company
www.hachette.co.uk

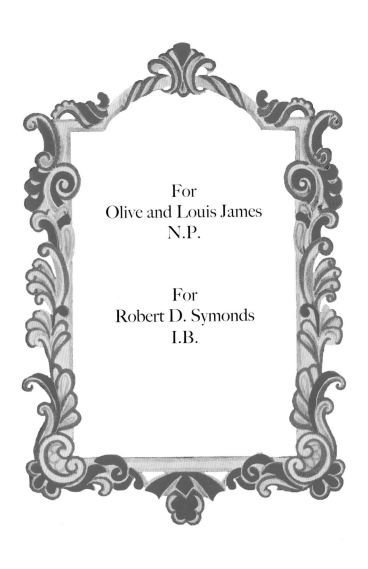

For
Olive and Louis James
N.P.

For
Robert D. Symonds
I.B.

Contents

INTRODUCTION

O N Sunday, 18 September 1825, the young Hans Christian Andersen – still a struggling and rather immature schoolboy at the age of twenty – confided to his diary: "I must carry out my work! I must paint for mankind the vision that stands before my soul in all its vividness and diversity; my soul knows that it can and will do this."

Though he was from a poor family and knew no one, this earnest young man had been taken up by some of Denmark's most influential people; the king himself approved a grant from a royal fund to provide his belated education, and future grants were to support the struggling writer.

Andersen's curious combination of hypersensitivity and unshakeable self-belief – nakedly displayed in *The Diaries of Hans Christian Andersen* (1990) – carried him through numerous false starts until he found the medium in which he could paint his vision for mankind: the fairy tale. In Andersen's hands this art form – the storytelling vehicle of the dreams and longings of the unlettered – became a subtle method of autobiography. Andersen himself takes the central role in nearly all his tales, whether disguised as a student, a gardener, a mermaid or a shirt collar; when he came to publish an actual autobiography, he entitled it *The Fairy Tale of My Life*.

In that book, Andersen recalls how as a child he often used to visit the spinning-room of the pauper hospital and asylum in Odense, Denmark, where he was brought up. The old women there, entertained by Andersen's childish prattle, rewarded him "by telling me tales in return; and thus a world as rich as that of *The Thousand and One Nights* was revealed to me". That rich world of the Danish folk tale – later harvested by collectors such as Evald Tang Kristensen, and analysed by folklorist Bengt Holbek in his book *The Interpretation of Fairy Tales* (1987) – formed the soil in which Andersen's creativity could flower.

In 1857, Andersen stayed with Charles Dickens in England for five weeks. Although the two men had great respect for each other, the visit was a strain – Dickens's daughter Kate cruelly but succinctly summed up the family's view when she recalled, "He was a bony bore, and stayed on and on." Dickens himself – scrupulously polite and attentive to his guest – relieved his feelings afterwards by sticking a notice on the dressing-room mirror which read, "Hans Andersen slept in this room for five weeks – which seemed to the family AGES!"

The main problem was that Andersen's spoken English was almost incomprehensible. Andersen's first translator, Mary Howitt, spitefully assured Dickens that in fact Andersen didn't know Danish either. There is an edge to this comment. Andersen's Danish is not the severe, highflown literary Danish of his day – it is raw and unpolished, and in it one is always aware of the speaking voice. This directness and informality, both of phrasing and rhythm, stem directly from the storytelling of the old women in the Odense spinning-room, and they are one of the reasons why Andersen's fairy tales have stayed so fresh and appealing.

This colloquial quality was not always apparent in Victorian translations such as Mary Howitt's, which gave Andersen's tales a genteel and overworked air; one of my aims in making these new versions of some of Andersen's finest tales is to follow modern translators such as R. P. Keigwin and Brian Alderson in capturing his relaxed and intimate storytelling voice.

Interestingly, Andersen *did* connect with the Dickens children, when he was able to tell them stories, not with his voice, but with his scissors. Henry Dickens recalled, "He had one beautiful accomplishment, which was the cutting out in paper, with an ordinary pair of scissors, of lovely little figures of sprites and elves, gnomes, fairies and animals of all kinds, which might well have stepped out of the pages of his books. These figures turned out to be quite delightful in their refinement and delicacy in design and touch."

Many of Andersen's paper cuttings survive: they can be seen at the H. C. Andersen Museum in Odense, or enjoyed in books such as Beth Wagner Brust's *The Amazing Paper Cuttings of Hans Christian Andersen* (1994). In *Little Ida's Flowers*, Andersen portrays himself as the student who entertains Ida with both stories and paper cuttings; the cuttings themselves play a key role in "The Steadfast Tin Soldier."

Stories such as *Little Ida's Flowers* and *The Little Match Girl*, which have always been among his most popular, have led some modern writers – for instance John Goldthwaite in *The Natural History of Make-Believe* (1996) – to criticize Andersen for his "sentimentality". Yet this "sentimentality" of Andersen's is a strange thing. At the heart of his vision of the world lies the ability to find comedy in tragedy. Story after story ends sadly in rejection, humiliation, or disappointment, yet they are saved from self-pity by the "salt" of Andersen's wit and by the acuteness of his observation.

That Andersen is essentially a poet of human suffering can be seen in one of his finest and most famous stories, *The Little Mermaid*. Andersen felt driven to write this original fairy tale, of which he wrote that while "only an adult can understand its deeper meaning" nevertheless "I believe a child will enjoy it for the story's sake." The story is now perhaps best known in Disney's more optimistic version – but the deeper meaning resides in Andersen's bleak and painful original.

The Little Mermaid was the first fairy tale in which Andersen attempted to explore his spiritual beliefs. A later story, *The Bell*, expresses his deep faith in the beauty and holiness of the world, and the promise of new life and redemption beyond it. In it, two boys, one "a king's son", the other a pauper, make their way by separate routes – one in sunshine, the other in shadow – to the same transcendent moment at the end of their (life's) journey.

Both of the boys in this strange and moving tale are depictions of Andersen himself – they reassure him, and us, that a humble beginning and a difficult path will not make any difference in the end. The story, published in 1842, looks back to 1819, Andersen's confirmation year – the year in which he met and played with a real king's son, Prince Frederik, the future King Frederik VII of Denmark. In later life Andersen and Frederik were on close terms; Elias Bredsdorff records in *Hans Christian Andersen: The Story of His Life and Work* (1975) that the king treated the storyteller "almost like an old friend".

In 1987, the Danish historian Jens Jørgensen published an extraordinary and controversial book entitled *H. C. Andersen: En Sand*

Myte (*H. C. Andersen: A True Myth*), in which he constructed an intricate web of circumstantial evidence to support his theory that Andersen was in fact the illegitimate son of King Christian VIII (Prince Frederik's father) and Countess Elise Ahlefeldt-Laurvig.

Jørgensen makes a good case both that such a child existed, and that Andersen himself was quite possibly "adopted" by his impoverished parents. He also establishes a pattern of royal and aristocratic patronage of the gawky pauper boy which suggests that someone important was keeping a weather eye out for the lad.

Though he does not firmly establish his theory as fact, Jørgensen does show that Andersen himself probably came to believe it. In a diary entry for 3 January 1875, the last year of his life, Andersen remarks how many letters he has received, then adds drily, "One has my name and address: King Christian the Ninth."

This intriguing theory, which caused a sensation in Denmark, has been rejected by some scholars, such as Elias Bredsdorff. But while it must be treated with caution, it does provide a fascinating new context in which to view the "fairy tale" of Andersen's life, and in which to read a story such as *The Bell*. Is it of significance that the boy is always described as "a king's son", never as "a prince"? Was Andersen imagining how much easier his life's path might have been, if his childish boastings that he was really "a changed child of noble birth" were true? If so, his conclusion is that the path in sunshine and the path in shadow lead to the same final destination.

It was about *The Bell* that Andersen made his famous comment that his fairy tales "lay in my mind like seed-corn, requiring only a mountain stream, a ray of sunshine, a drop of wormwood, for them to spring forth and burst into bloom".

Nearly two hundred years after his birth, his garden of fairy tales is still in full flower.

NEIL PHILIP

THUMBELINA

ONCE there was a woman who longed for a child of her own, but she didn't know how to get one. So she went to an old witch and asked her, "Can you tell me where I can find a little child? I would so love one."

"That's easy," said the witch. "Take this barleycorn – but mind, it's not the sort that grows in the fields, or that you feed to the chickens. Put it in a flowerpot, and you shall see what you shall see."

"Oh, thank you!" said the woman, and she gave the witch a silver coin. Then she went home and planted the barleycorn, and right away it sprouted into a large, handsome flower that looked like a tulip. The petals were closed in a tight bud.

"What a lovely flower!" said the woman, and she kissed the red and yellow petals. As she kissed them, they snapped open. You could see that it was a real tulip, but right in the heart of the flower there sat a tiny little girl, so pretty and delicate that she was no bigger than the woman's thumb. So she called her Thumbelina.

A beautiful polished walnut shell served as her bed; she lay on violet petals, with a rose petal for her cover. That was where she slept at night; but in the daytime she played on the table, where the woman set out a soup bowl filled with water, with flowers wreathed around the edge. The stalks dangled in the water. A large tulip petal floated on the surface, and Thumbelina could sit on that and row from one side to the other, using two white horsehairs as oars. She looked such a fetching sight! And she could sing, too, in the prettiest voice you ever heard.

One night, as she lay in her beautiful little bed, an ugly old toad hopped in through a broken window pane. It was a horrid, slimy thing, and it jumped right down onto the table where Thumbelina lay sleeping under her red rose petal.

"She would make just the wife for my son," said the toad. And she grabbed the walnut shell in which Thumbelina was sleeping and hopped away with it, back through the window and into the garden.

At the bottom of the garden there was a wide stream, and it was on the muddy, marshy bank that the old toad lived with her son. He was a fright, just like his mother! "*Koax, koax, brekke-ke-kex*," was all he could say, when he saw the pretty little girl in the walnut shell.

"Don't make such a noise, or she'll wake," said the old toad. "She might easily run away from us, for she's as light as swan's-down. Let's put her out in the stream, on one of those great water-lilies; she's such a slip of a thing, she'll think it's an island. She can't get away from there, and in the meantime you and I can prepare the best room under the mud, where you and she will make your home."

There were many water-lilies in the stream, with broad leaves that floated on the surface. The biggest of them all was the furthest out, and the old mother toad swam out to it, and left Thumbelina there in her walnut shell.

Early next morning the poor little thing woke up, and when she saw where she was she began to weep bitterly, for the leaf was surrounded by water and there was no way to reach the bank.

19

The old toad had been busy in the mud, decorating a room with rushes and marsh marigolds, to make it all bright and snug for her new daughter-in-law. Then she swam out with her son, to fetch Thumbelina's walnut shell bed, so that they could set it up ready in her room. The old toad curtseyed to Thumbelina from the water, and said, "Well, this is my son! He's to be your husband, and I'm sure you'll be very happy together, in your lovely home beneath the mud."

"*Koax, koax, brekke-ke-kex*," was all the son could say.

Then they took the neat little bed and swam away with it. Thumbelina, left alone on the green leaf, sat and wept. She did not want to live with the horrid old toad, or marry her ugly son.

The little fishes swimming in the water had heard what the toad said, and they poked their heads up to catch sight of the little girl. As soon as they saw her, they were won over by her beauty. They couldn't bear to think that she must marry the ugly toad and live in the mud. It must not be! They gathered round the green stalk that held up the water-lily leaf, and nibbled at it till it gave way.

The leaf floated downstream, with Thumbelina aboard; it carried her far away, where the old toad could never follow.

Thumbelina sailed on past all sorts of places, and the wild birds in the trees sang out, "What a pretty creature!" as she passed. On and on, farther and farther floated the leaf; and that was how Thumbelina set out on her travels.

A pretty white butterfly kept fluttering round and round her, till at last it settled on the leaf, for it was quite taken by the little girl. And she too was happy, now she had escaped from the toad. Everything was so beautiful. The sunshine on the water shone like burnished gold. She took off her sash and tied one end to the butterfly, and the other to

the leaf. Then she sailed even faster.

Just then a big cockchafer-beetle came buzzing by. As soon as he saw her, he snatched her round her slender waist with his claw, and flew up into a tree with her. But the green leaf still floated down the brook, and the butterfly had to go with it, because he was tied to the leaf and couldn't get loose.

Oh! How frightened Thumbelina was when the cockchafer carried her up into the tree! And she was sad, too, for her poor dear butterfly;

for unless he could manage to free himself from the leaf, he would surely starve. But that didn't bother the cockchafer. He settled beside her on the largest leaf in the tree, and fed her honeydew from the blossoms. He told her she was lovely, although she wasn't a bit like a cockchafer.

By and by all the cockchafers who lived in the tree came to give her the once over. The young lady cockchafers shrugged their feelers, and said, "She's only got two legs, the miserable creature! She hasn't any feelers! With that pinched little waist she might almost be a human. How ugly she is!" That's the kind of thing they said.

The cockchafer who had carried her off thought she was beautiful, but when all the others kept saying how ugly she was, he began to believe them. At last he would have nothing more to do with her; she could go where she pleased. They flew her down from the tree, and set her on a daisy. There she sat and wept, because she was so ugly that the cockchafers didn't want to know her; yet really she was as pretty as can be – as perfect as a rose petal.

All summer long poor Thumbelina lived alone in the greenwood. She plaited grass blades together to make a bed, and hung it under a large dock leaf to shelter from the rain. She ate the nectar from the flowers, and drank the dewdrops from the leaves; and so the summer and the autumn passed.

Then came winter – the long, cold winter. All the birds who had sung to her so sweetly flew away; the trees lost their leaves and the flowers withered. Even the big dock leaf under which she lived curled up into a faded yellow stalk. Poor Thumbelina was terribly cold, for her clothes were in rags, and she was so small and frail. It seemed she would freeze to death.

When it began to snow, every snowflake buffeted her like a shovelful thrown on us; for remember she was no bigger than your thumb. She wrapped herself up in a withered leaf, but there was no warmth in that. She trembled with cold.

On the edge of the wood lay a large cornfield. The corn had been harvested long before; only the hard bare stubble remained, sticking out of the frozen earth. But that was like a forest for Thumbelina to travel through – and oh! How she shook with cold.

At last she came to a field-mouse's house. The field-mouse had made herself a snug home in a hole beneath the stubble. There was a storeroom full of corn, and a warm kitchen, and a dining room. Poor Thumbelina stood like a beggar-girl at the door, and asked if she might have a piece of barleycorn, for she hadn't eaten a thing for two whole days.

"You poor mite!" said the field-mouse, for she had a kind heart. "Come into the warm and eat with me."

She took a great liking to Thumbelina, so she said, "Why don't you stay here with me? Just keep my room neat and tidy, and tell me stories, for I am very fond of stories." And Thumbelina did as the good old field-mouse asked, and made herself comfortable.

"We shall have a visitor soon," said the field-mouse. "He lives nearby, and he pops in every week. His house is even bigger than mine, with huge rooms, and he wears a gorgeous black velvet coat. Now he would be a catch as a husband, although his eyesight's not good. You must save all your best stories for him."

Thumbelina paid no attention to this, for she had no thought of marrying him, however many times the field-mouse told her how rich and clever he was, and what a big house he had – twenty times larger than hers. He was a mole; and he came to call in his velvet suit. He knew about all sorts of things, but he couldn't abide the sunshine or flowers – though he never saw them. Thumbelina had to sing for him. She sang "Ring a ring o' roses" and "I had a little nut tree", and the mole fell in love with her because she sang so sweetly. But he didn't say anything, because he was such a cautious sort.

He had dug a long passage from his house to theirs, and he told them that they could walk in it whenever they liked. They were not to be afraid of the dead bird that was lying there. It was a whole bird, with its beak and feathers intact, and he supposed it must have died recently, at the start of winter, and been buried where he had made his underground passage.

The mole took a piece of rotten wood in his mouth – for in the darkness, that shines just like a torch – and led the way down the long dark passage. When they came to the place where the dead bird lay, he thrust his broad snout up through the earth, to let in some light. In the middle of the floor lay a swallow, his wings clenched to his sides, and his head and legs tucked beneath his feathers. The poor bird must have frozen to death.

Thumbelina felt so sorry, for she loved all the birds that had sung so delightfully for her all through the summer. But the mole just kicked it aside with his stumpy legs, saying, "That one's chirped its last chirp! Who'd be born a bird? Thank goodness no child of mine will ever suffer that fate! A bird can't do anything but tweet, and when winter comes it starves to death."

"That's the sensible view," said the field-mouse. "What does a bird have to show for all its twittering when winter comes? It must starve and freeze. I can't see what people see in them."

Thumbelina said nothing, but when the other two had turned their backs on the bird, she stooped down to smooth aside the feathers that covered his head, and kissed his closed eyes. "Who knows?" she thought. "This may be the very one that sang so beautifully to me last summer."

The mole stopped up the hole he had made for the daylight, and saw the ladies home. But that night Thumbelina could not sleep. So she got up, and wove a covering out of hay, and took it and spread it over the dead bird; and she took some soft thistledown from the field-mouse's room and tucked the bird in, to keep it warm under the cold earth.

"Goodbye, dear bird," she said. "Goodbye, and thank you for your lovely song in the summer, when all the trees were green, and the sun was so warm." And then she laid her head on the bird's breast. That gave her a terrible fright, for it seemed something was beating inside. It was the bird's heart. He was not dead, he had fainted away, and now that he was warmer, he revived.

In autumn, the swallows all fly away to the warm countries; but if one lingers behind, it freezes and falls down as if it were dead. And there it lies, and the cold snow covers it.

Thumbelina was trembling with fright, for the bird was so much bigger than she, who was no bigger than a thumb. But she gathered her courage, and tucked the bird in even tighter, and fetched a mint leaf that she had been using as a coverlet and laid that over his head.

That night she stole down to the bird again, and this time he was more himself, though still very weak. He opened his eyes for a moment to look at Thumbelina, standing there with a piece of rotten wood in her hand, for she had no other light. "Thank you, you dear child," said the sick swallow. "I'm warm again now, and soon I shall be strong enough to fly out in the bright sunshine."

"Oh!" said Thumbelina. "It's so cold out now! It's snowing and freezing. You stay here in the warm; I will take care of you."

Then she brought the swallow some water in a leaf, and as the bird drank he told her how he had torn one of his wings on a thorn bush and so had not been able to keep up with the other swallows when they flew away to the warm countries. At last he had fallen to the ground; after that, everything was blank. He didn't know how he came to be where he was.

The swallow stayed in the passage all winter. Thumbelina looked after him, and became very fond of him. But she didn't say anything to the mole or the field-mouse, for she knew that they did not care about the poor swallow.

As soon as spring came, and the sun began to warm the earth, the swallow said farewell to Thumbelina, who opened up the hole that the mole had made in the roof of the passage. The sun was so welcome as it flooded in; the swallow asked Thumbelina if she would like to come with him. She could sit on his back, and they would soar away into the greenwood. But Thumbelina knew that the old field-mouse would be hurt if she left like that.

"No, I can't," she said. "I mustn't."

"Then farewell, farewell, you dear kind girl," said the swallow, and he flew away into the dazzling sun. Thumbelina's eyes filled with tears as she watched him go, for she had come to love the swallow.

"*Tweet, tweet!*" sang the bird, and flew off into the greenwood.

Thumbelina was so sad. She wasn't allowed to go out into the warm sunshine, and anyway in the field above the corn grew so tall that it seemed like a dense forest to the little girl, who was only the size of a thumb.

"You must get your wedding trousseau ready this summer," said the field-mouse. "You shall have clothes in linen and wool – the best of everything, for when you are married to the mole."

So Thumbelina had to spin the wool, and the field-mouse hired four spiders to weave for her, day and night. Every evening the mole came visiting, and the only thing he could talk about was how the summer was coming to an end, and once the sun had stopped scorching the earth so dry, he and Thumbelina would be married. This didn't make Thumbelina happy, for she did not care for the boring old mole.

Every morning, as the sun rose, Thumbelina would creep out of the door. When the wind bent the tops of the corn aside, she could see the blue sky, and she thought how beautiful and bright it was, and longed to see the swallow once more. But the bird never came; he must have been flying in the greenwood.

Then it was autumn, and Thumbelina's trousseau was ready.

"Only four more weeks, and you shall be married!" said the field-mouse. But Thumbelina broke down in tears, and said that she did not

want to marry that dull mole.

"Hoity-toity!" said the field-mouse. "Don't take on such airs, or I shall bite you with my white teeth. Why, the mole will make you a splendid husband. He's handsome – why, the queen herself hasn't got a black velvet coat to match him. And he's rich – with the finest kitchen and cellar. You should be thankful."

The wedding day arrived. The mole was to come early, to fetch Thumbelina. She was to live with him, deep down under the earth, and never come out into the bright sunshine, for he didn't like it. The poor child was heartbroken at having to say goodbye to the beautiful sun. At least while she was living with the field-mouse she had been able to glimpse it from the doorway.

"Goodbye, bright sun!" she cried, lifting her arms up to it; and she took a few steps out into the open. The corn had been harvested, and once again the stubble was left. "Goodbye, goodbye!" she repeated, and she threw her arms round a little red poppy that was growing there. "Give my love to the swallow, if ever you see him."

"*Tweet, tweet!*" she heard overhead. It was the swallow! He was so pleased to see Thumbelina. But she was crying. She told him how she must marry the mole, and live underground where the sun never shone. She hated the thought.

"The cold winter will soon be here," said the swallow. "I shall fly away to the warm countries. Will you come with me? You can sit on my back, and tie yourself on with your sash. We'll fly far away from the stupid mole and his gloomy house – right across the mountains, to where the sun shines hot, and the flowers are in bloom because it's always summer. Come and fly with me, dear Thumbelina, who saved my life when I lay frozen in the dark passage under the earth."

"Yes, I'll come with you!" said Thumbelina. And she climbed onto the bird's back, resting her feet on his wings, and tying herself to one of the strongest feathers with her sash. Then the swallow soared high into the air, and flew away over the forest and lake, and across the high mountains where the snow always lies. Thumbelina shivered in the keen frosty air; but she snuggled down in the bird's warm feathers, with just her head peeping out to gaze on the beauty below.

At last they came to the warm countries. The sun was shining much more brightly than at home, and the sky seemed twice as high. On the terraced slopes were growing green and purple grapes; there were lemons and oranges; the scent of myrtle and sweet herbs hung in the air. Laughing children ran about the ways, chasing bright butterflies. But the swallow kept on flying, and the countryside below seemed to grow even more beautiful.

Beside a still blue lake, in the shade of tall trees, stood the ruins of an ancient palace, built of white marble long ago. Vines trailed round its pillars, and at the very top there were swallows' nests. One of these belonged to the swallow on whose back Thumbelina was riding.

"This is my home," cried the swallow. "But if you would rather live on the ground, you can choose the most beautiful flower of all, and make your house there."

"That would be lovely!" said Thumbelina, and she clapped her tiny hands.

A great white column lay fallen on the ground. It had broken into three pieces, and between these there grew the most gorgeous white flowers. The swallow flew down with Thumbelina, and set her on one of the broad petals – and what a surprise she got! There, at the heart of the flower, sat a little man, so fair he was almost transparent, as if he were made of glass. He was wearing a tiny gold crown on his head, and fine, shining wings on his shoulders; he was no bigger than Thumbelina. He was the flower fairy. Each of the flowers had such a spirit living in it, and he was the king of them all.

"How handsome he is!" breathed Thumbelina to the swallow.

The fairy king was at first quite alarmed at the bird, which seemed a giant compared to him; but when he saw Thumbelina he was enchanted, for she was the loveliest girl he had ever seen. So he took the gold crown off his head and placed it on hers. He asked her what her named was, and if she would marry him, and be queen of all the flowers.

This was a husband Thumbelina could truly love – not like the old toad's ugly son, or the blind dull mole in his black velvet coat. So she said yes to the handsome king.

Then all the flower fairies came out of their flowers – each one so dainty and graceful, and each one with a gift for Thumbelina. Best of all was a pair of beautiful wings. They were fastened to her shoulders, and now she too could fly from flower to flower. Everyone rejoiced; and the swallow, sitting in his high nest, sang his sweetest song – though he was sad, too, for he loved Thumbelina, and didn't want to part from her.

"You shall not be called Thumbelina any more," said the king of the flowers. "It's an ugly name, and you are so pretty. We shall call you Maia."

"Farewell, farewell," sang the swallow, and he flew away from the warm countries, far away back to Denmark. There he had a little nest by the window of a man who writes fairy tales. "*Tweet! tweet!*" sang the swallow. And the man listened, and he wrote down this story.

LITTLE IDA'S FLOWERS

"**M**Y poor flowers are nearly dead!" said little Ida. "Only last night they were so beautiful, and now they are withering." She showed them to the student who was sitting on the sofa. She was very fond of him, because he used to tell her wonderful stories and could cut amazing pictures out of a piece of paper – hearts with little dancers in them, flowers, and great castles with doors that opened. He was a lighthearted young man.

"Why are they drooping so?" she asked.

"Don't you know?" replied the student. "They've been dancing all night. They are exhausted; that is why they are hanging their heads."

"But flowers can't dance," said Ida.

"Oh yes they can," said the student. "After dark, when we are all tucked up in our beds, the flowers hop around quite gaily. They hold a ball nearly every night."

"Can their children go to the ball, too?" asked Ida.

"Yes, both the daisies and the lilies-of-the-valley can go."

"And where do the loveliest flowers dance?"

"Do you remember the flower garden of the king's summer palace, where you go to feed bread to the swans? That's where the grand ball is held."

"I went there yesterday with Mother," said Ida. "But there wasn't a leaf on the trees, and there were no flowers at all. Where can they have gone? There are so many in the summertime."

"The king and queen move to the city for the winter, and as soon as they have gone, the flowers move into the palace and have a wonderful time. You should see them! The two loveliest roses go and sit on the throne and act the king and queen. The red cockscombs line up along both sides and bow, like gentlemen of the court. Then all the most beautiful flowers come in, and the grand ball begins. The blue violets are young naval cadets, and they dance with the hyacinths and crocuses, whom they call Miss. The tulips and the big yellow lilies are like old dowagers, and they keep an eye on things and make sure there's no hanky-panky."

"But," interrupted Ida, "surely the flowers aren't allowed to hold a ball in the king's palace."

"Nobody knows anything about it," said the student. "Once in a while the old night watchman who looks after the castle walks through it, but he carries a bunch of keys, and when they hear the keys rattling, all the flowers hide. Sometimes the night watchman sniffs the air, and thinks to himself, I'm sure I can smell flowers, but he has never seen them."

"Oh, what fun!" said little Ida, and she clapped her hands. "But could I see the flowers?"

"Of course," said the student. "Next time you are there, just peep through the windows, and you'll be sure to see them. Only today I saw a long yellow daffodil reclining on a sofa, pretending to be a lady-in-waiting."

"What about the flowers in the botanical garden – could they go to the ball? It's a long way."

"Yes, they could. If flowers really want to, they can fly. That's what butterflies are – flowers that jumped off their stems, flapped their petals, and flew away. Some of them never go back to their stems but grow real wings and flutter about all day. You must have often seen it.

"It may be that the flowers in the botanical garden have never heard what goes on in the palace. Next time you are there, lean over and whisper to one of the flowers, 'There's a grand ball at the summer palace tonight,' and then just wait and see. Flowers can't keep a secret; they'll whisper it from one to another, and at nightfall they'll all fly away. The professor who looks after them will go into the garden and find all the flowers gone. That will give him something to think about!"

"But how can the flowers tell each other about the ball? They can't speak."

"Not in words," said the student. "They communicate by mime. You must have seen them nodding and swaying in the breeze. They can understand each other just as well as we can by talking."

"Does the professor understand them?" asked Ida.

"He most certainly does! Why, one morning he went into the garden and saw a hulking great stinging nettle rustling its leaves at a pretty little red carnation. It was saying, *I love you, dreamboat.* Now the professor doesn't like that kind of talk, so he rapped the nettle over its fingers – its leaves, you would call them. But the nettle stung him, and ever since the professor has been afraid to touch a nettle."

Ida laughed. "What fun!"

But the grumpy old councillor who was also sitting in the room said, "Fancy filling a child's head with such rubbish!" He didn't like the student one bit. When the student made one of his funny papercuts –

it might be of a man hanging from a gallows with a heart in his hand, who had been condemned for stealing hearts, or an old witch riding on a broomstick, with her husband balanced on her nose – the councillor would always mutter, "Such rubbish to put into a child's head! What tomfoolery!"

But Ida thought what the student had said was very funny, and she kept on thinking about it. She was sure that the flowers were hanging their heads because they were tired out from dancing all night. She took them over to the little table where her playthings were, and where her doll Sophie was sleeping in her cradle. Ida said, "You must be a good doll, Sophie, and let the flowers sleep in your bed tonight, for they are ill and need to be made better. You can sleep in the drawer." Sophie never said a word, but she looked cross at having to give up her bed to the flowers.

Ida laid the faded flowers in her doll's bed, tucked them in, and told them to lie quiet while she made them a cup of tea. "You'll feel much better in the morning," she said. Then she drew the curtains around the bed so that the sun wouldn't shine in their eyes.

All that evening she kept thinking about what the student had told her. At bedtime, she went to the window and peeped behind the curtains at her mother's tulips and hyacinths in their pots, and whispered, "I know where you are going tonight." The flowers acted as though they hadn't understood; they never stirred a leaf. But Ida knew what was what.

Once she was in bed, Ida lay awake thinking how lovely it would be to see the beautiful flowers dancing in the king's palace. *I wonder if my flowers have really been there?* she thought, and then she was asleep.

In the middle of the night, she woke; she had been dreaming about the flowers, and how the councillor had scolded the student for filling her head with rubbish. It was very quiet in her bedroom; the night-light was burning on the table beside her; her mother and father were asleep.

I wonder if my flowers are still lying in Sophie's bed, she thought. *I would love to know!* She sat up in bed and looked through the open door to the room in which the flowers were. She thought she could hear a piano playing, soft and sweet.

Now all the flowers are dancing. Oh! If only I could see them! But she didn't dare get up, for fear of waking her mother and father.

If only they would come in here! she thought. But the flowers never came, though the beautiful music kept playing. She couldn't bear it any longer. She crept out of bed, tiptoed to the door, and looked into the next room.

There was no night-light, but it wasn't dark, because the moon was shining through the window onto the floor. It was nearly as bright as day. All the tulips and hyacinths were standing in two long rows on the floor; they had left their flowerpots behind on the windowsill. The flowers danced so prettily on the floor, holding on to each other's leaves and swinging each other around.

A tall yellow lily was playing the piano. Ida remembered seeing it in the garden that summer, because the student had said, "It looks just like Miss Lena!" And although everyone had laughed at him then, Ida now thought that the flower did look just like Miss Lena; it had the same trick of turning its face from side to side as it played, and nodding in time to the music.

None of the flowers noticed little Ida.

Now a tall blue crocus leaped right up onto the table and drew back

39

the curtains from the cradle where the sick flowers were lying. They looked quite well again, and they wanted to join in. The old porcelain chimney sweep with the chipped chin stood up and bowed to them, and then they were swept off into the dance.

Something fell from the table with a crash. It was a bundle of sticks tied together with ribbons into a switch, which had been given to Ida for a carnival parade. It thought it was a flower too; and it did look fine, with its ribbons flying. It had three legs, and it could dance the mazurka, which none of the flowers could do because they couldn't stamp.

Now there was a little wax doll tied to the top of this switch, wearing a wide-brimmed hat just like the councillor's. All at once, this doll seemed to swell up, and it boomed, "Fancy filling a child's head with such nonsense! What tomfoolery!" It really did look just like the councillor, and Ida couldn't help laughing.

The switch kept dancing all this time, and whipping at the wax doll with its ribbons, so that the doll had to dance too, until the softhearted flowers begged it to stop.

Then came a knocking from the drawer. The little porcelain chimney sweep managed to open it a crack, and Sophie the doll poked her head out. "Is there a ball going on? Why wasn't I told?"

"May I have the pleasure of this dance?" asked the sweep.

"You? Dance with me?" said Sophie, and she sat down on the open drawer with her back to him. She thought that one of the flowers would ask her to dance; but none of them did. The chimney sweep had to dance on his own, and he didn't do badly at all.

Sophie coughed – *ahem! ahem!* – but still none of the flowers noticed her. So she let herself fall to the floor. She landed with a crash,

and all the flowers ran up to her to ask whether she had hurt herself;
Ida's flowers were especially concerned. But Sophie wasn't hurt in the
slightest. Ida's flowers said thank you for the loan of the bed, and
Sophie said they were quite welcome, and she was perfectly happy in
the drawer. Then all the flowers danced around her in the middle of the
floor, where there was a great splash of moonlight.

Sophie told the flowers they could keep her bed, but they replied,
"Thank you, but we shan't need it. We don't live long; we shall be
dead by the morning. Ask Ida to bury us in the garden, where the
canary is buried. Next year we shall come to life again, and be even
prettier."

"You mustn't die," said Sophie, and she kissed the flowers.

At that moment the door of the drawing room opened, and a troop of
lovely flowers came dancing in. Ida could not think where they could
have come from, if not from the king's palace. Two beautiful roses
wearing crowns led the way. They were the king and queen. Behind
them came the stocks and carnations, bowing to the company. There
was even a band – poppies and peonies blowing on the pods of sweet
peas until they were red in the face, and bluebells tinkling like real
bells. It was a funny sort of orchestra.

At the end of the throng came all the dancing flowers – violets,
daisies, lilies-of-the-valley. It was lovely to see how they kissed each
other at the end of the dance.

At last they said goodnight to one another, and little Ida crept back
to bed, to dream of everything she had seen.

Next morning when she woke, she ran straight to the doll's cradle to
see if the flowers were still there. They were, but they had withered
and died. Sophie was still in the drawer; she looked very sleepy.

"Do you have something to tell me?" asked Ida; but Sophie just looked stupid and didn't say a word.

"You're very naughty," said Ida, "and yet all the flowers danced with you." Then she took a cardboard box with a picture of a bird on it and laid the flowers in it, saying, "When my cousins come from Norway, we shall bury you in the garden, so that you will come up again next year."

Ida's cousins were two lively boys called Jonas and Adolph. Their father had given them new bows and arrows, and they brought those with them to show Ida.

She told them all about the poor dead flowers, and the two boys came to the funeral. They walked in front, with their bows slung over their shoulders, and Ida followed with the dead flowers in their pretty coffin. They dug a hole in the corner of the garden. Then Ida kissed the flowers, and she laid them in the ground in their box. As they didn't have a gun or a cannon, Jonas and Adolph shot arrows over the grave.

THE WILD SWANS

FAR away, where the swallows fly in winter, lived a king who had eleven sons, and one daughter, Elise. The eleven brothers went to school with stars on their breasts and swords at their sides. They wrote on golden slates with diamond pencils, learned all their lessons off by heart; you could tell they were princes. Their sister Elise used to sit on a shining glass stool, reading a picture book that cost half a kingdom. The children had all they could want; but it didn't last.

Their father the king married a wicked queen, who was not well-disposed to the poor children – they found that out on the very first day. There was a big party at the palace, and the children played their old game of pretending to be visitors. But the queen did not give them any cakes or baked apples, as usual. She just handed them a teacup full of sand, and told them to feed their imaginations on that.

A week later, she sent little Elise to the country to be brought up by peasants, and it was not long before she had filled the king's head with so many lies about the poor princes that he turned against them.

"Fly away, out into the world, and look after yourselves," said the wicked queen. "Fly away as great, voiceless birds." But for all her ill-will, she couldn't do them as much harm as she wished; for they turned into eleven beautiful wild swans. With a strange cry, they flew out of the castle window, across the park, and over the wood.

It was still early in the morning when they passed over the cottage where their sister Elise was sleeping. They hovered over the roof, flapping their great wings and stretching their long necks, but no one heard or saw them. They had to fly off again, up in the clouds, and out into the world. At last they came to a wide, dark forest that ran all the way down to the sea.

Poor Elise was left in the peasant's cottage, with only a green leaf to play with. She pricked a hole in it and peeped through it at the sun, which made her think of her brothers' bright eyes; and whenever the sun fell warm upon her face, she thought of her brothers' kisses.

One day passed like another. When the wind blew through the rose hedge in front of the cottage, it whispered to the roses, "Is there anyone more beautiful than you?" and the roses would nod their heads, and answer, "Elise." And when the peasant's wife sat in the doorway of a Sunday, reading her hymn book, the wind used to turn the pages, and ask the book, "Is there anyone more faithful and pure than you?" and the book would rustle its answer, "Elise." And it was all true, what the roses and the hymn book said.

When Elise was fifteen, she had to go home. When the queen saw how beautiful Elise had grown, she hated her. She would have liked to turn her into a wild swan like her brothers, but she did not dare, because the king wanted to see his daughter.

So the next morning the queen went into her bathroom, which was made of marble, but softly carpeted, with cushions everywhere. She fetched three toads, kissed them, and said to the first one, "Sit on Elise's head when she gets into the bath, so that she will turn dull and stupid like you." To the second one she said, "Sit on Elise's forehead, so that she will turn ugly and loathsome like you, and her father won't know her." And to the third she whispered, "Sit on Elise's heart, and fill her with wicked thoughts to torment her." Then she put the toads in the clear water, which at once turned brackish and green.

She called Elise, undressed her, and made her get into the bath. The first toad sat on her head, the second on her forehead, and the third on her heart. But Elise did not seem to notice them.

When Elise got out of the bath, three red poppies were left floating on the water. If the toads had not been poisonous, and kissed by a witch, they would have been turned into roses as they rested on Elise's head and heart; she was too good to be hurt by any witchcraft.

When the wicked queen realized this, she rubbed walnut-juice all over the girl's body, and smeared a vile, smelly ointment all over her face, and tangled her beautiful hair. When the king saw her, he was horrified, and said it couldn't possibly be his daughter. No one wanted to know her, except for the old watchdog, and the swallows, and their opinions didn't count.

Poor Elise wept, and thought of her eleven brothers, who had all disappeared. With a troubled heart, she crept out of the castle and walked all day over fields and moorland till she reached the forest. She didn't know where she was going, but she was so sad, and she missed her brothers so much. They must have been cast out just like her, and she made up her mind to find them.

She had not been long in the forest when night fell. She was lost in the dark, so she lay down on the soft moss, said her evening prayer, and rested against a tree trunk. It was very still in the forest, and the night air was soft. All around gleamed the green fire of hundreds of glow-worms. When Elise idly touched a branch above her, the shining

insects fell about her like shooting stars.

All night long she dreamed about her brothers. They were all
children again, playing together, and writing on their gold slates with
their diamond pencils, or looking at the pictures in the beautiful book
that had cost half a kingdom – but this time they weren't just copying
letters onto the slates, as they used to. They were writing down all the
brave deeds they had done, and the bold adventures they had had. And
in the picture book, everything had come alive – the birds sang, the

people stepped out of the pages and talked to Elise and her brothers. But when she turned a leaf, they jumped back in again, so the pictures didn't get muddled.

When Elise awoke, the sun was already high. She couldn't see it properly through the trees, but the sunbeams danced through the dense branches in a shimmering haze. There was a fresh, green smell, and the birds almost came and perched on her shoulders. She could hear the sound of water splashing; there were several springs flowing into a pool. Elise made her way down to the water, by a path that had been worn through the undergrowth by deer going for a drink. The water was so clear that if the wind hadn't disturbed the trees and bushes she might have thought they were painted on the water – every leaf was so sharply reflected, whether it was the sunshine or the shade.

When Elise saw her face reflected in the water she got a shock – it didn't look like her at all. But she dipped her hand in the water, and rubbed her eyes and forehead till she could see her own face again. Then she took off her clothes, and stepped into the fresh water to bathe. In the whole world there was no one as lovely as Elise.

When she had dressed, and plaited her hair, she went to the bubbling spring and drank from her cupped hands. Then she carried on into the forest, though she still did not know where she was going. She thought of her brothers, and of God who would surely not forsake her. It was he who made the wild apples grow, so that the poor would not go hungry. Here was just such a tree, heavy with fruit.

Elise ate a midday meal beneath its shade, and afterwards propped up the groaning branches. Then she walked on, into the darkest part of the wood. It was so still she could hear her own footsteps, and even the rustling of the withered leaves as she trod them underfoot. No bird was

to be seen, and not a single ray of sun could pierce through the thick foliage. The tall tree trunks were so close together it looked as though she were completely enclosed by interlaced branches. Oh, this forest was a lonely place!

And the night was so dark! Not a single glow-worm showed its light. Sad and forlorn, she lay down to sleep. And it seemed to her that the branches above her parted, and that God watched over her gently, with angels crowding to peep over his shoulders. In the morning when she woke she did not know if this was a dream.

She walked on a short while, and met an old woman with a basket full of berries; the old woman gave her some. Elise asked if she had seen eleven princes riding through the forest.

"No," said the old woman, "but yesterday I saw eleven swans with gold crowns on their heads, swimming down by the river near here." And she led Elise to a hill, at the foot of which a river was winding. The trees on each bank leaned over the water to touch each other; with the effort, the roots had wrenched themselves from the earth to trail out over the water.

Elise said goodbye to the old woman, and followed the river till she came to the place where it met the sea.

The great, endless ocean lay before her. But there was not a ship or a boat to be seen – how could she go on?

She gazed at the countless pebbles on the beach, worn smooth by the waves: glass, iron, stone, all had been shaped and subdued by the water, though this was softer even than Elise's delicate hand. "The waves just keep rolling," she said, "making the rough stones smooth. I will be just as tireless. Thank you for your lesson, you bright waves. Some day, my heart tells me, you shall carry me to my dear brothers."

Scattered on the seaweed at the tide-line, Elise found eleven white swans' feathers, which she carefully gathered up. Drops of water clung to them – whether they were dew, or tears, Elise couldn't tell. She was quite alone on the shore, but she didn't mind, for the sea was always changing. The sea changes more in an hour than a lake does in a year. If a black cloud passed overhead, the sea seemed to say, "I can frown, too," and then the wind would get up, and ruffle the waves white; when the sky flushed pink, and the wind dropped, the sea could look just like a rose petal. It was now green, now white. It was never full at rest; for always along the shore there was a gentle heave and swell, like the breathing of a sleeping child.

At sunset, Elise saw eleven wild swans with golden crowns on their heads flying in from the sea; they streamed one after another through the air like a long winding ribbon. Elise hid behind a bush, while the swans settled near her, flapping their great white wings.

As the sun sank below the horizon, the swans' feathers suddenly fell away, and there stood eleven handsome princes, Elise's brothers. She uttered a sharp cry: for though they were much changed, she knew them at once – she was sure they were her brothers. She ran to their arms, calling their names. They were overcome with joy to recognize their sister, who had grown so tall and beautiful. Between laughter and tears, the story was soon told of how wickedly their stepmother had treated them.

"As long as the sun is in the sky," said the eldest of the brothers, "we fly as wild swans. But when the sun has set, we regain our human form. So we must take care at sunset to reach dry land: for if we were out riding the air, when we became human we should fall to our death. We don't live here. Across the sea there is a land just as beautiful as this, but it's a long way there. We must cross the wide ocean, where there is no island for us to rest overnight – just one lonely little rock sticks up above the waves, just big enough for us to stand side by side. There we spend the night, in human form, and when the sea is rough, the spray soaks us; but we are thankful for that little rock. Without it, we could never return to visit our own country.

"We can only come once a year, for we need two of the longest days for our flight. We can only stay eleven days, but during that time we can fly over this forest, from which we can see the castle where we were born, and where our father lives, and also the tower of the church in which Mother is buried. Here, we feel at home with the trees and bushes; here, the wild horses gallop across the plain, as they did in our childhood; here, the charcoal-burner sings the old songs we heard in our childhood; we are drawn here, and here we have found you, our dear sister. We may stay here two days more, then we must fly back across the sea, to a fine land, though not our own. How can we take you with us? We have neither ship nor boat."

"And how shall I free you?" asked Elise. And they talked it over through the night; they only had a few hours' sleep.

Elise was woken by the whirring of swans' wings overhead. Her brothers were again transformed; they were flying above her in wide circles. At last they flew far, far away – but one of them, the youngest, stayed behind. The swan laid his head in her lap, and she stroked his white wings; they stayed like that all day. As the day wore on the others returned, and when the sun set they were all standing on the firm land in their human form.

"Tomorrow we shall fly away, and cannot return for a whole year – but we cannot leave you. Dare you come with us? Between us we must surely have enough strength in our wings to carry you across the sea."

"Yes, take me with you," said Elise.

They spent the whole of that night weaving a net from supple willow bark and tough rushes, till it was really strong. Elise lay down on it, and when the sun rose, the brothers were again transformed into wild swans, they seized the net in their beaks and flew high into the clouds with their dear sister, who was still asleep. The sun's rays shone full on her face, so one of the swans flew above her, to shade her with his outstretched wings.

They were far from land when Elise awoke. She thought she was still dreaming, so strange did it seem to her to be carried through the air, high above the sea. By her side she found some ripe berries, and tasty roots, which the youngest of the brothers had gathered for her. She thanked him with a smile, for she knew that he was the one flying overhead, and shading her with his wings.

They flew so high that the first ship they saw beneath them looked like a white seagull skimming over the water. Behind them, on a huge white cloud as big as a mountain, Elise could see giant shadows of herself and the eleven swans. Never before had she seen such a splendid picture – but as the sun rose higher, and they left the cloud behind, the shadow picture disappeared.

All day long they whizzed through the air like arrows – yet not so fast as usual, because they had their sister to carry. A storm was brewing, and evening was approaching. Elise watched anxiously as the sun went down; still there was no sign of the lonely rock. She thought the swans were beating their wings even more furiously. Oh! It was all her fault if they were not flying fast enough. When the sun set, they would become human beings again, and then they would fall into the

sea and be drowned. She prayed to God from the bottom of her heart, but still she could not see the rock. The black clouds gathered; the gusting winds heralded a storm. The waves seemed turned to lead, and in the clouds lightning flashed.

The sun was now on the rim of the ocean. Elise's heart thumped. Then, all of a sudden, the swans darted downwards – so quickly she thought she was falling – but the next moment they were hovering. The sun was half below the horizon. At that moment she saw the little rock below; it looked like a seal's head raised above the water. The sun was sinking fast; now it was as small as a star. As her foot touched the solid rock, the sun winked out, like the last spark on a piece of burning paper, and there were her brothers, standing arm in arm around her. There was only just room for her and them – no more. The sea dashed itself against the rock, drenching them in a shower of foam; the sky was ablaze with the glare of lightning, and thunder crashed. Elise and her brothers kept hold of each others' hands, and sang a hymn, which comforted them and gave them courage.

By daybreak, the air was pure and still, and as soon as the sun rose, the swans flew off with Elise from the rock. There was still a strong sea running, and as they looked down from the clouds the white-flecked waves seemed like millions of swans swimming on the dark green sea.

When the sun was high in the sky, Elise saw in front of her, floating in the air, a land of mountains and glaciers. In the very middle was a palace. Below it, palm trees waved, and gorgeous flowers as big as mill-wheels. She asked if this was their destination, but the swans shook their heads. What she saw was the ever-changing cloud palace of the fairy Morgana, which no mortal could enter. Even as she looked, the mountains, and the palm trees, and the palace vanished, and in their place rose twenty high-towered churches. She thought she could hear an organ playing, or was it the sea? As she got near to the churches, they changed into a fleet of ships sailing below. She looked down – and all she could spy was a sea-mist drifting across the ocean.

At last she caught sight of the beautiful blue mountains of the land for which they were heading. Cedar woods, towns, and castles rose into view. And at sunset, Elise was sitting on a mountain side, in front of a large cave that was so overhung with delicate green creepers that they looked like embroidered curtains.

"I wonder what you will dream of tonight," said the youngest brother, as he showed her where to sleep.

"If only I could dream how to set you free!" she answered.

She could think of nothing else. She prayed so hard; yes, even in her dreams she was praying. And it seemed to her that she flew high up through the air, to Morgana's cloud palace. The fairy welcomed her. She was dazzlingly beautiful, yet somehow she reminded Elise of the old woman who had given her berries in the forest, and told her of the swans with golden crowns.

"You have the power to set your brothers free," she said. "But have you the courage and the determination? Is it true that the sea is softer than your fair hands, and yet can mould hard stones to its will. But the sea cannot feel the pain your fingers will feel; and the sea has no heart to feel the fear and grief that you will suffer.

"Do you see this stinging nettle in my hand? There are many such growing by the cave in which you sleep; only those, and the ones that grow in the churchyard, are any use – remember that. You must gather them, though they will burn blisters on your skin. Then you must tread

on them with your bare feet, to break them into flax. This you must
weave into eleven shirts with long sleeves. Throw them over the eleven
wild swans, and the spell is broken. But remember – from the moment
you begin your work until it is finished, even if it takes years, you
must not speak. The first word that falls from your lips will strike like
a dagger at your brothers' hearts. Remember!"

And then the fairy touched Elise's hands with the nettle. It burned
like fire, and she awoke.

It was broad daylight. Close by lay a nettle just like the one she had
seen in her dream. She knelt down in thanks to God, and went out of
the cave to begin her work. She plucked the stinging nettles with her
delicate hands, though they seared her skin, burning great blisters on
her hands and arms. She did not mind the pain, if it would set her
brothers free. She trampled the nettles with her bare feet, and woven
them into green flax.

At sunset her brothers returned. They were worried when they found
Elise so silent; they thought it must be some new spell of the wicked
stepmother's. But when they saw her blistered hands, they realized
what she was doing for their sake. The youngest brother wept, and
where his tears fell on burned hands the pain was soothed.

That whole night Elise worked without rest. How could she rest
until her brothers were free? All next day she worked alone, while the
swans flew far away; never had time passed so quickly. As soon as the
first shirt was finished, she began on the second.

Suddenly a hunting horn rang out among the hills. Elise was
frightened. The noise came nearer; now she could hear the baying of
the hounds. In terror she fled into the cave. She tied the nettle-yarn into
a bundle, and sat on it.

At that moment a huge hound sprang out of the bushes; then another, then another. They kept barking and running to and fro. Soon the hunters were outside the cave; the handsomest of them all was the king of the land. He stepped up to Elise; never had he seen such a beautiful girl.

"How did you come here, fair maid?" he asked. Elise shook her head; she didn't dare to speak, for a single word would cost her brothers their lives. She hid her hands under her apron, so that the king should not see her suffering.

"Come with me," he said. "You cannot stay here. If you are as good as you are beautiful, I will dress you in velvet and silk. I will put a gold crown on your head, and you will live in my palace." He lifted her onto his horse. She wept and wrung her hands, but he said, "I only want to make you happy. You will thank me one day." And away he rode across the mountainside, holding her in front of him, and the rest of the hunt following on.

As the sun set, the domes and spires of the splendid royal city lay before them. The king took Elise to the palace. Fountains were playing in the high marble hall, and the walls and ceiling were covered with beautiful paintings. But Elise had no eyes for such things – her eyes were blinded by tears. She let the waiting women dress her in royal clothes, and weave pearls into her hair, and draw long soft gloves over her blistered hands.

As she stood there in such rich clothes, her beauty was so overpowering that the courtiers all bowed low before her, and the king chose her for his bride, even though the archbishop shook his head, and muttered that this pretty wood sprite much be a witch, to enchant everybody so, and enthrall the king.

But the king wouldn't listen. He called for music, and a feast, and dancing girls. Elise was led through sweet-scented gardens into a magnificent apartment, but still she grieved. Nothing brought a smile to her lips, or a light to her eyes.

Then the king showed her the little room where she was to sleep. It was hung with a costly green tapestry, and looked much like the cave where she had been found. On the floor lay the bundle of flax she had spun from the nettles, and on the wall hung the shirt that she had already finished. One of the hunters had brought it all along.

"Here you can dream you are back in your old home," said the king. "Here is the work you were doing. Sometimes, amid all this grandeur, it may amuse you to think of the old days."

When Elise saw these things that were so dear to her heart, she smiled, and the blood returned to her cheeks at the thought that she might still save her brothers. She kissed the king's hand; he hugged her to his heart, and ordered the church bells to chime out the news of their wedding. The lovely silent maiden from the woods was to be queen of all the land.

The archbishop whispered his malice into the king's ear – but not into his heart. The wedding went ahead, and the archbishop himself had to crown her. Out of spite he forced the narrow circlet down so hard that it hurt. But sorrow made such a tight ring round her heart – sorrow for her brothers – that she never noticed the pain.

She remained silent, for a single word would cost her brothers' lives; but the light from her eyes told the king that she returned his love. She grew fonder of him every day. If only she dared tell him of her sorrow! But she must remain silent, until her work was done. Therefore she used to steal away every night, to the little room that was fitted out like the cave, and weave the shirts. But just as she was beginning the seventh, she ran out of flax.

She knew that the right kind of nettles grew in the churchyard, and that she must gather them herself. But how was she to bear it?

"What is the pain in my fingers compared to the agony in my heart?" she thought. "I must try. God will not forsake me."

Then, as fearful as if she were creeping out to form some evil deed, she crept down into the moonlit garden, through long avenues and empty streets until she reached the churchyard. There she saw, sitting on one of the big tombs, a group of fearsome witches. They were stripping off their rags as if to bathe, and digging with their bony fingers into the newmade graves; they were scrabbling out the corpses and feasting on their flesh. Elise had to pass right by them, and they fixed her with their eyes; but she said a prayer, gathered the stinging nettles, and carried them back to the palace.

Only one person had seen her – the archbishop. He was on the watch, while others slept. Now he was certain: the queen wasn't what she appeared. She was a witch, who had enchanted the king.

In the confessional, he told the king what he had seen, and what he feared. When the false words fell from his lips, the carved saints shook their heads, trying to say, "It's not true. Elise is innocent!" But the archbishop said that they were shaking their heads in horror.

Two great tears rolled down the king's cheek. He went home with a troubled heart. At night he pretended to sleep, but sleep never came; he noticed Elise slip from her bed every night, and he followed her in secret, and saw her go into the little room.

Day by day his looks darkened. Elise noticed, but she couldn't think why. It fretted her; and besides, her heart was heavy with sorrow for her brothers. Her salt tears ran down onto her velvet dress of royal purple; they lay there like sparkling diamonds, so that everyone who saw her said, "How wonderful! I wish I were queen!"

Now she had nearly completed her task. There was only one shirt left to make, she didn't have a single nettle left. So one last time she must venture to the churchyard and gather the final few handfuls. She shivered at the thought of that lonely walk, and those awful witches, but her will was set as strong as her trust in God.

Off she went; the king and the archbishop followed her. They saw her disappear through the churchyard gates. As they entered, they saw the haglike witches sitting on the tomb, just as Elise had seen them. The king turned away, for he thought she must be one of them – his own Elise, whose head had rested upon his breast that very evening. "Let the people judge her!" he said; and the people condemned her to be burned at the stake.

She was dragged to a dark damp cell, where the wind whistled through a barred window. Instead of velvet and silk, they gave her the nettles she had gathered; these must be her pillow. The shirts she had woven must be her blankets. But they couldn't have given anything more precious to her, and she continued to work, praying hard all the time. Outside, children in the street sang jeering songs about her; not a soul had a word of comfort or kindness for her.

Then, as evening fell, she heard the beating of swans' wings at the grating. It was the youngest of her brothers, who had found her at last. She sobbed aloud for joy, although she knew that the coming night might be her last. For her work was nearly done, and her brothers were near.

The archbishop came to keep her company in the final hours; he had promised the king to do that. But she shook her head, and made signs for him to go. That night she must finish her task, or all her suffering – the agony, the tears, the sleepless nights – would have been in vain. The archbishop went away, with cruel words. But Elise knew she was innocent, and went on with her work.

Little mice scurried about the floor, dragging the nettles to her to help her; a thrush sat on the windowsill all night, and sang as merrily as he could, to keep up her spirits.

It was still twilight; the sun would not rise for an hour. There stood the eleven brothers at the palace gate, demanding to see the king. But they were told that could not be. It was night; the king was still asleep; they dared not wake him. The brothers begged, and threatened. The guard was called. At last, the king himself turned out to find out what was going on. But at that moment the sun rose, and the brothers could not be seen – just eleven white swans flying over the palace.

The people poured out of the city gates, eager to see the witch burned. One poor nag pulled the cart in which Elise sat. She was dressed in a coarse dress made of sacking; her beautiful long hair hung limply over her shoulders; her cheeks were pale as death; her lips were moving gently as she wove the green flax. Even on the road to death she would not give up her work. The ten shirts lay at her feet, and she worked at the eleventh, while the rabble mocked and jeered.

"Look at the witch, mumbling away! That's no hymn book in her hands, but some witch's work. Take it from her, and tear it up!"

And they all crowded round her to tear but what she had made. But eleven white swans came flying down, and settled on the cart, flapping their great wings. The crowd were terrified.

"It's a sign from heaven!" some whispered, though they didn't dare say it aloud. "She must be innocent."

The executioner took her by the hand – but she quickly threw the eleven shirts over the swans, and they turned into eleven handsome princes. Only the youngest had a swan's wing instead of one arm, for his shirt was missing a sleeve – it had not been finished.

"Now may I speak!" she cried. "I am innocent."

And the people, who had seen what had happened, bowed down to her as to a saint. But Elise, worn out by worry, fear, and grief, sank back lifeless into her brothers' arms.

"Yes, she is innocent," said her eldest brother. And he told them all what had happened. As he spoke, a wonderful fragrance filled the air. For every piece of wood in the fire built around the stake had taken root, and sent forth branches, until they made a high hedge around Elise, full of red roses. At the very top there was a single pure white flower, bright as a shining star. The king plucked it, and laid it on Elise's breast; and she awoke, with peace and joy in her heart.

The church bells rang out, and the air was filled with flying birds.

What a joyous parade it was back to the palace! No king could command anything so fine.

THE SWEETHEARTS

A whipping top and a ball were lying in a drawer along with some other toys. The top said to the ball, "Shouldn't we be sweethearts? After all, we are lying right next to each other in the drawer." But the ball, who was made of morocco leather, thought herself too much of a lady even to notice such a comment.

Next day, the little boy whose toys they were came and painted the top red and yellow and hammered a brass nail into its middle, so the top looked really splendid when he spun around.

"Look at me!" he said to the ball. "What do you say now? Shouldn't we be sweethearts? We'd be so good together – you leaping, and me dancing. No one would be happier than us."

"That's your opinion," said the ball. "You don't seem to realize that my mother and father were a pair of morocco slippers, and that I have a cork inside me."

"Yes," said the top, "but I am made of mahogany. The mayor himself turned me on his own lathe, and he was very pleased with me."

"Oh yes?" said the ball. "And I'm supposed to believe that?"

"May I never be whipped again, if I spoke a word of a lie," said the top.

"You speak very well for yourself," replied the ball, "but I can't accept you – for I am as good as half engaged to a swallow. Every time I go up in the air, he pops his head out of his nest, and says, 'Will you? Will you?' and I have made up my mind to say yes – and that's as good as half engaged. But I do promise that I shall never forget you."

"That's a big help," said the top, and after that they had nothing more to say.

The next day the ball was taken out. The top watched as she flew up in the air like a bird, until she was out of sight. Every time she came back down, and when she hit the ground she bounced up high again – which was either because she wanted to, or because she had a cork inside her.

The ninth time the ball went up, she didn't come down again. The boy searched all over for her, but she was gone.

"I know where she is," sighed the top. "She's in the swallow's nest. She's going to marry the swallow."

The more the top brooded on this, the more he longed for the ball. Because he couldn't have her, he loved her more than ever. How could she choose another? It was a real puzzle. The top spun and whirled around, and all the time he was thinking about the ball. In his imagination she grew prettier and prettier. The years went by, and she became his lost love.

The top wasn't young any more – but then one day he was painted all over with gold. He was better than new; for now he was a golden top. He whizzed around and sprang into the air for joy. That was something! But then he jumped too high and was gone.

They looked for him high and low, but they couldn't find him. Where on earth was he?

He had jumped into the garbage can, where there was all kinds of

rubbish – cabbage stalks, floor sweepings, and the contents of the gutters.

This is a fine mess I've landed myself in, thought the top. *My gilding won't last long in here. What a lot of riffraff.* He glared at a long cabbage stalk that was poking too near him, and at a strange round thing like a rotten apple. But it wasn't an apple, it was an old ball, that had lain for years in the sodden ooze of the gutter.

"Thank God! Someone to talk to at last!" said the ball, looking at the golden top. "I am made from morocco leather, and was sewn by a fine young lady, and I have a cork inside me – though you might not think so to look at me. I was going to marry a swallow, but I fell into the gutter, and I have been lying there for the past five years in the ooze. And you know, that's a long time for a young girl."

The top didn't reply. He thought of his old sweetheart, and the more he heard, the more he felt that this was she.

Then the maid came to throw something away. "Hey! Here's the golden top!" she shouted.

And the top was brought back into the house, where he was greeted with delight. No one spoke of the ball, and the top never mentioned his lost love again.

That's how it goes, when your sweetheart has lain five years in the gutter. You don't know her when you meet her in the garbage.

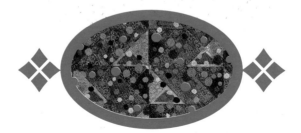

THE NIGHTINGALE

Y OU know that in China the Emperor is Chinese, and all the people around him are Chinese too. This story happened a long time ago, which is all the more reason I should tell it to you now, before it is forgotten.

The Emperor's palace was the finest in the world, made entirely of the most delicate porcelain, so precious and so fragile that you had to be very careful about touching anything. The garden was full of rare flowers, and the loveliest had little silver bells tied to them, that tinkled to attract the attention of passers-by.

Yes, everything in the Emperor's garden was very well thought out, and it stretched so far that even the gardener had no idea where it ended. If you kept on walking you came at last to a beautiful wood, with tall trees and still lakes. The wood went right down to the sea, which was blue and deep; big ships could sail right in under the high branches of the trees.

Among those branches lived a nightingale, who sang so sweetly that even the poor fisherman, with all his cares, would stop to listen while casting his nets each night. "It does my heart good to hear it," he would say; but then he had to get on with his work, and forget the bird.

Yet the following night he would stop again to listen to her song: "It does my heart good."

Folk came from all over to admire the Emperor's city, his palace, and his garden; but when they heard the nightingale, they all said, "That's the best of all." And when they returned home, they never forgot the bird when telling their tales, so that when learned men wrote books about the city, the palace, and the garden, the nightingale always got the highest praise; poets wrote lovely poems about the nightingale in the wood by the sea.

These books went all over the world, and one of them at last reached the Emperor. There he sat in his golden chair, reading away; every now and then he nodded his head, to show how pleased he was with the splendid descriptions of his city, palace, and garden. "But best of all is the nightingale," said the book.

"What's this?" said the Emperor. "The nightingale? Why, I've never heard of it. Can there really be such a bird in my empire – in my own garden – and no one told me? Fancy having to find it out from a book."

So he called for his lord-in-waiting. This gentleman was so grand that whenever anyone of lower rank dared to speak to him, he only answered "Pah!" which doesn't mean anything much.

"It says here that we have a most remarkable bird, called a nightingale," said the Emperor. "Her song is supposed to be the finest thing in all my empire. Why have I never been told about her?"

"I have never heard of her," said the lord-in-waiting. "She's never been presented at court."

"It is my wish that she should be brought here tonight to sing for me," said the Emperor. "The whole world knows about this treasure of mine except for me!"

"I have never heard of her," repeated the lord-in-waiting. "But she shall be found."

But where? The lord-in-waiting ran upstairs and downstairs, along the corridors and back again, but none of the people he questioned had ever heard of the nightingale. So the lord-in-waiting hurried back to the Emperor and said that it must be a story invented by the writer of the book. "Your Majesty must not believe everything you read. These writers make it all up – the artful rogues."

"This book" said the Emperor, "was sent to me personally by the high and mighty Emperor of Japan, so it cannot be untrue. I *will* hear the nightingale, and I will hear it tonight! If she fails to appear, immediately after supper every courtier shall be punched in the stomach."

"*Tsing-Pe!*" said the lord-in-waiting, and he ran upstairs and downstairs, along the corridors and back again, this time with half the court at his tail, for they didn't fancy the idea of being punched in the stomach directly after supper. Everywhere, they asked about this nightingale, who was known to all the world except the court.

At last they came across a poor little kitchen-maid, who said: "Oh yes, the nightingale! I know her well. How she sings! Every evening I take some scraps from the table to my poor sick mother, who lives by the shore. On my way back, I rest in the wood, and the nightingale sings to me. It brings tears to my eyes, as if mother was kissing me."

"Little kitchen-maid," said the lord-in-waiting, "if you can take us to this nightingale, you shall have a proper job in the kitchen, and be allowed to watch the Emperor at his dinner. For the Emperor has commanded her presence at court."

So they all went to the wood where the nightingale sang. On the

way, they heard a cow moo. "Ah, there she is!" cried the courtiers. "What a powerful voice for such a small bird! Yes, we've heard her before."

"That is a cow mooing," said the little kitchen-maid. "There's still a long way to go."

Then some frogs began to croak in the pond.

"Divine!" said the Emperor's chaplain, "Just like church bells!"

"No, those are frogs," said the little kitchen-maid, "but I expect we will hear her soon."

And then the nightingale began to sing.

"There she is," cried the little girl. "Listen! Listen! She's up there." And she pointed to a drab little bird up in the branches.

"Is it possible?" said the lord-in-waiting. "Who would have thought it? How plain she is. But perhaps she is abashed by such distinguished visitors."

"Little nightingale," called the kitchen-maid, "our gracious Emperor would like you to sing for him."

"With all my heart," said the nightingale, and at once she began to trill and sing.

"It's like glass bells chiming," said the lord-in-waiting. "See how her throat moves! It is extraordinary we've never heard of her before; she'll be a great hit at court.''

"Shall I sing once more for the Emperor?" said the nightingale, who thought that the Emperor must be one of the visitors.

"Most excellent nightingale," replied the lord-in-waiting, "it is my privilege to summon you to a concert at the court tonight, where you will enchant His Imperial Majesty with your delightful song."

"It sounds best among the green trees," said the nightingale, but she went with them willingly when she heard that that was what the Emperor wanted.

The whole palace had been scrubbed and polished, till the porcelain walls shone in the light of thousands of gold lamps. The loveliest flowers were arranged in the corridors, with bells tied to them, that tinkled in the air stirred by servants scurrying to and fro – you could hardly hear yourself think.

In the middle of the great hall where the Emperor sat, a golden perch was put up for the nightingale. The whole court was there, and the little kitchen-maid had special permission to stand behind the door, now that she had the official title Imperial Kitchen-Maid. Everyone was dressed up in all their finery, and all eyes were on the plain little bird.

The Emperor nodded; that was the signal to begin.

The nightingale sang so beautifully that it brought tears to the Emperor's eyes; they actually rolled down his cheeks. At that, the nightingale's song grew even lovelier – it touched the hearts of all who heard. The Emperor was so delighted that he said the nightingale should have his gold slipper to wear around her neck but she said no thank you, she already had her reward. "I have seen tears in the Emperor's eyes, and that is all the reward I ask. There's a strange power in an Emperor's tears." And then the nightingale sang again.

"She's quite bewitching!" sighed the ladies of the court; and they each took a gulp of water and tried to gurgle it in their throats, to see if they could be nightingales too. Even the lackeys and chambermaids were pleased, and that's saying a lot because they're the hardest audience of all. No doubt about it, the nightingale was a great hit.

So the nightingale was to stay at court, and have her own cage, with

permission to fly out twice each day, and once each night. But whenever she flew, she had twelve attendants holding tight a silk ribbon tied round her leg, so there wasn't much fun in it.

Still, she was the talk of the town. When two people met, one would say "night" and the other would answer "gale," and that was all that needed to be said. Eleven new babies were called Nightingale, though none of them could sing a note.

One day, a large parcel arrived for the Emperor. On it was written NIGHTINGALE.

"This must be a new book about our famous bird," said the Emperor. But it wasn't a book. It was a mechanical toy in a box – an artificial nightingale. It looked just like the real one except it was covered all over with diamonds, rubies, and sapphires. All you had to do was wind it up and it would sing one of the songs that the real bird sang; and all the while its tail bobbed up and down, glittering with silver and gold. Round its neck hung the message, "The Emperor of Japan's nightingale is a poor thing beside the nightingale of the Emperor of China."

"How wonderful!" they all exclaimed. The man who had brought the present was given the title Imperial Nightingale Bringer.

"Let's hear them together," someone said. "What a duet that will be!"

So the two birds sang together, but it wasn't a success. For the real nightingale sang in her natural way, while the artificial bird sang by clockwork. "And none the worse for that," said the Imperial Music Master. "She keeps perfect time; she knows the rules."

After that, the artificial bird sang by itself. It was just as popular as the real one, and so much better looking.

Over and over it sang its song – thirty-three times and never got tired. Everyone wanted it to sing again, but the Emperor said it was time for the real nightingale to have a turn.

But where was she? She had flown away to the greenwood out of an open window, and no one had noticed.

"Dear, dear, dear," tutted the Emperor. "Is this the thanks I get?" And all the courtiers agreed that the nightingale was the most ungrateful creature, and called her names.

"At any rate," they said, "we have the better bird here." So the clockwork bird had to sing once more. This was the thirty-fourth time they had heard the very same tune; but it was very difficult, so they didn't notice.

The Imperial Music Master praised the bird very highly; it was better than the real bird in every way – not just because of the jewels on the outside, but for the clockwork on the inside. "You see, ladies and gentleman, and above all Your Imperial Majesty, with the real nightingale you could never tell what was coming, but with the artificial bird it's all pre-arranged. You know what you will hear. Open it up, and you can see the thinking: how the wheels turn to grind out the notes."

Everyone agreed. The Imperial Music Master got permission to show off the new bird to the public on the following Sunday. "They must hear it sing," said the Emperor. And hear it they did. It made them quite tipsy; they all said, "Oh!" and wagged their fingers in the air, and nodded their heads. Only the poor fisherman who used to listen to the real nightingale said, "It's like, yet . . . not like. There's something missing, though I can't put my finger on it."

The real nightingale was banished from the empire.

The artificial bird lived on a silken cushion by the Emperor's bed;
all the presents it received, gold and precious stones, lay beside it; it
was made Chief Imperial Bedside Minstrel, First Class on the Left –
even Emperors keep their hearts on the left.

The Imperial Music Master wrote a book in twenty-five volumes all
about the artificial bird, using the longest and most difficult words he
could find; everyone pretended to have read it and understood it, for no
one wants to be thought stupid.

This went on for a year, until the Emperor, his court, and all his
subjects, knew by heart every trill of the toy bird's song; but that only
made them like it all the more, as they could sing along. The boys in
the street sang, "*Zi-zi-zi*! *Kluk-kluk-kluk*!" and the Emperor sang it, too.
It was great fun.

But one evening, when the artificial bird was in full song, and the
Emperor was lying in bed and listening, something went, "Snap!"
inside the bird. *Whirr-rr-rrr-*. The wheels whizzed round, and the
music stopped.

The Emperor sprang out of bed, calling for the doctor – but what
could he do? Then they fetched the watchmaker, and with a lot of
muttering and poking he managed to get the bird going after a fashion;
but he said it mustn't be used too often, as the clockwork was almost
worn out, and it couldn't be repaired.

It was all very sad. Once a year the artificial bird was allowed to
sing, and even that was a struggle. Still, the Imperial Music Master
made a speech full of long words, saying the bird was as good as ever,
so of course it must have been.

Five years passed, and a great sorrow fell on the empire. The people
really were fond of the Emperor, and now it was reported that he was

ill, and close to death. A new Emperor had already been chosen, and when people in the street asked the lord-in-waiting for news, he just said "Pah!" and shook his head.

Cold and pale lay the Emperor in his magnificent bed. The whole court regarded him as dead already, and had rushed off to greet the new Emperor; the lackeys were standing around gossiping, and the chambermaids were all drinking tea. Heavy cloth had been laid down on all the floors to deaden the noise; the whole palace was still, so still.

But the Emperor wasn't dead yet. He lay, pale and unmoving, in his great bed with its heavy velvet curtains and its golden tassels; through an open window, the moonlight shone down on the Emperor and the clockwork bird.

The poor Emperor could scarcely breathe; he felt as if something were sitting on his chest; he opened his eyes, and saw that it was Death, wearing the Emperor's gold crown and holding in one hand the Imperial sword and in the other the Imperial banner. All around the bed, in the folds of the velvet curtains, were strange faces – some kind and friendly, some hideous and hateful. They were the Emperor's good and evil deeds, clustered around him, as Death sat on his heart.

"Do you remember this?" they whispered, one after another. "Do you remember that?" They went on and on, until the sweat broke out on the Emperor's forehead.

"I never knew" cried the Emperor. "I didn't realize." Then he called out, "Music! Music! Sound the great drum, so I can't hear what they're saying!" But still they went on, and Death nodded his head at every word.

"Music! Music!" pleaded the Emperor. "Beautiful little golden bird, I beg you, sing! I've given you gold and precious stones; I've hung my golden slipper round your neck. Sing, please, sing!"

But the bird was silent. There was no one there to wind it up, and it could not sing without that. Death just stared at the Emperor with his great hollow eyes, and everything was still, so still.

All at once, by the window, the sweetest song rang out. It was the living nightingale, sitting on a branch outside. She had heard of the Emperor's illness, and come to bring him what comfort she could. And as she sang, the ghostly faces grew fainter and fainter; the blood began to pulse more strongly through the Emperor's feeble limbs; even Death listened in, and said, "Go on, little nightingale, go on!"

"Yes if you'll give me that fine sword . . . yes, if you'll give me that splendid banner . . . yes, if you'll give me the Emperor's gold crown."

And Death gave up each treasure for a song. The nightingale went on singing. She sang of the quiet churchyard where the white roses bloom, and the elderflowers smell so sweet, and the green grass is watered with tears. She filled Death with longing for his garden, and in a cold white mist he floated out of the window.

"Thank you, thank you!" said the Emperor. "You heavenly little bird. I remember you. I banished you from my lands, yet you have sung away those terrible phantoms from my bed, and lifted Death from my heart. How can I ever repay you?"

"You have already given me my reward. When I first sang to you, I saw tears in your eyes; that, I shall never forget. Those are the only jewels I value. But sleep now, and wake refreshed, and strong. I will sing you a lullaby."

And the nightingale sang, and the Emperor fell into a sweet sleep – such a calm, peaceful sleep.

When the sun woke him, shining through the window, he was

himself again. None of his servants had bothered to come; they all thought him dead. But the nightingale was still there, still singing.

"You must stay with me for ever," said the Emperor, "but only sing when you want to. As for the artificial bird, I shall break it into a thousand pieces."

"Don't do that," said the nightingale. "It did its best. Keep it. As for me, I can't live in a palace. Let me come when I like, and sit in the evening on this branch by your window, and sing to you – happy songs, and sad songs, too. I will bring you news of joy and sorrow – everything that happens, good and bad, in your lands – news that has always been kept from you. For this little bird flies far and wide; I visit the fisherman's hut and the peasant's cottage, far from you and your court. I love you for your heart, not for your crown – yet the crown has its own magic. I shall come, and sing to you. But you must promise me one thing."

"Anything!" said the Emperor. He was standing, dressed in his Imperial robes, and holding the Imperial sword against his heart.

"All I ask is this. Tell no one that you have a little bird that brings you all the news; then all will be well. "And the nightingale flew away.

The servants came in to have a look at their dead master. They stopped in their tracks!

"Good morning," said the Emperor.

THE BELL

A T sunset, when the clouds glowed gold between the chimneys, the narrow streets of the city would be filled with a strange sound like the tolling of a church bell. People would hear it for a moment, and then the rumbling of the carts and the general hubbub would drown it out. "That's the evening bell," people said. "The sun's going down."

On the outskirts of the city, where the houses were spaced apart and had gardens and fields around them, the sunset was even lovelier, and the tolling of the bell was much louder. It seemed to come from a church in the heart of the still, fragrant forest. People would look in that direction, and feel quiet and thoughtful.

As time passed, one person would say to another, "Is there a church in the woods? The bell has such a strange, lovely sound. Why don't we go and look for it?"

The rich people drove in their carriages, and the poor people walked, and to all of them the road seemed very long. When they finally came to a clump of willows that grew on the edge of the forest, they sat down under the trees. Looking up into the branches, they thought they were right out in the wilds. A baker from town pitched a tent and began to sell cakes; soon there were two bakers, and the second one hung a bell over his tent. It was covered in tar to protect it from the weather, and it had no clapper.

When the people got back to town they said it had all been very romantic; and that was worth the effort, even without the tea party. Three of them said they had gone right to the other side of the forest. They could still hear the bell, but now it seemed to be coming from the city. One wrote a whole poem about it. He said the bell was like a mother's endearments to her child; no melody could be sweeter than that bell's song.

At last the emperor heard about it, and he promised that whoever could find out where the sound came from should have the post of "Ringer of the World's Bell" even if it turned out not to be a bell at all.

So more and more people went looking for the bell, for they wanted the job. Only one came up with an explanation. He hadn't been much further into the wood than the rest, but he claimed that the bell sound came from a great owl in a hollow tree. It was the owl of wisdom, and it kept knocking its head against the trunk. He just wasn't sure whether the sound came from the bird's head or from the tree trunk. So he was made Ringer of the World's Bell, and every year he published an essay on the owl, without leaving anyone the wiser.

And now it was Confirmation Sunday. The priest had spoken so well and sincerely that the young people were all deeply moved. This was a big day for them, the day they became grown-ups. Their child-souls had to become adult and sensible.

It was beautifully sunny outside, and after the service the children who had been confirmed walked out of the city. From the forest came the powerful tolling of the big, unknown bell. They were filled with the desire to go and look for it – all except three. One of them was a girl who had to hurry home to try on her ballgown, for it was because of the dress and the ball that she had been confirmed that day; otherwise she wouldn't have come. Another was a poor boy who had borrowed both his suit and his shoes from the landlord's son, and had to take them back straight away. The third said he never went to strange places unless his parents were with him, and as he had always been a good boy, he was going to carry on being one even after he was confirmed. That's nothing to make fun of – but they all did.

So three of them stayed behind, but the others went on. The sun shone, the birds sang, and the young people sang, too. They walked hand in hand, for as they hadn't taken their places in the world yet, they were still children in the eyes of heaven.

Soon two of the smallest grew tired and turned back to town, and two girls sat down to make wreaths of wild flowers. When the rest arrived at the willow trees where the bakers had their tents, they said, "Well, here we are! Now we can see that there isn't really a bell. People just imagine it."

Just then, from deep in the woods, the bell rang out, pure and true. Five of the children made up their minds to carry on into the forest. It was hard going, for the trees grew so thickly, and the flowers grew so tall. Flowering convolvulus and brambles trailed in long garlands from tree to tree; the nightingale sang, and the sunbeams played. Oh, it was beautiful; but it was no place for girls, for their dresses would be torn to bits.

They came to some great boulders covered in different kinds of moss. A fresh spring was gurgling up, glug, glug.

"I wonder if that might be the bell," said one of the five, lying down to listen. "This needs looking into." So he stayed behind, and the others went on.

They came to a cottage made of branches and bark. A huge crab-apple tree was leaning over it, and roses were growing up it and over the roof. From one of its branches hung a little bell. Was that the bell they had heard? They all agreed it was, except for one boy who said that this bell was too small and delicate to be heard so far away, and that its tinkling tones could never touch the heart so deeply. But he was a king's son, and the other said, "His kind always has to know better than anyone else."

They let him go on alone. As he went on, his heart was more and more filled with the loneliness of the forest. He could still hear the little bell that the others were so pleased with, and even, when the wind was in the right direction, the sound of singing from the tea party at the baker's tent. But the tolling of the great bell sounded ever louder; it reverberated like an organ, and it came from the left, where the heart is.

There was a rustling in the bushes, and there before the king's son stood a boy wearing wooden clogs and a jacket with sleeves so short that you couldn't help noticing his bony wrists. They recognized each other; it was the boy who couldn't join the others after the Confirmation service because he had to return his suit and shoes to the landlord's son. Now he had followed alone in his clogs and old clothes, so strong was the pull of the deep-tolling bell.

"Let's go on together," said the king's son. But the poor boy tugged at his sleeves and stared at his clogs. He mumbled that he was afraid he wouldn't be able to keep up. Besides, he thought that the bell should be looked for on the right, where everything great and glorious is.

"Then we shan't meet again," said the king's son, nodding to the poor boy, who disappeared into the densest part of the wood, where brambles and thorns would tear his old clothes to shreds and scratch his face, hands, and feet until they bled. The prince, too, got scratched, but his path lay in the sunshine. We'll follow him, for he was a bold lad.

"I will find the bell," he said, "if I have to go to the ends of the earth."

Hideous monkeys up in the trees bared their teeth in a grin and chattered to each other, "Shall we pelt him? Shall we pelt him? He's the son of a king."

But he kept on walking deeper and deeper into the forest. There, the most wonderful flowers grew: lilies like white stars, with blood-red stamens; tulips as blue as the sky, that sparkled in the wind; and apple trees with fruit like shining soap bubbles. How those trees must have glittered in the sun! He passed green meadows where deer roamed on the grass beneath oak and beech trees, and every crack in the tree bark was filled with grass and moss. There were also woodland glades with peaceful lakes on which swans swam gracefully and flapped their wings. Often the king's son stopped to listen, thinking that the sound of the bell might be coming from one of these deep lakes, but no, it was from yet deeper in the wood that the tolling came.

Now it was sunset. The sky was red as fire, and the forest grew so still that the boy flung himself to his knees. He sang an evening hymn, and said, "I'll never find what I'm looking for. The sun is setting, and night is coming; soon it will be dark. But perhaps if I climb up those rocks, which are higher than the tallest trees, I may get one last glimpse of the round, red sun."

By catching hold of roots, he pulled himself up the wet rocks, past writhing snakes and toads that seemed to bark at him.

He reached the top just as the sun set. Oh, what magnificence! The sea, the boundless sea, stretched out before him, dashing its waves against the shore. Over where the sea met the sky stood the sun, like a great, shining altar. Everything fused together in the golden glow. The forest sang, the ocean sang, and his heart sang, too. All nature was a great holy cathedral. The trees and the floating clouds were the pillars; the flowers and grass were the woven altar cloth; and heaven itself was the dome.

The glory faded as the sun went down, but millions of stars were kindled, like so many diamond lamps. The king's son spread out his arms to it all: sky, ocean, forest. At that moment, from the right, came the poor boy in his outgrown jacket and wooden clogs. He had arrived almost as quickly, by going his own way.

The two boys ran to each other. They stood together, hand in hand, in the great cathedral of nature and poetry, and the sacred invisible bell tolled its joyful hallelujah above them.

THE SNOW QUEEN
A Story in Seven Parts

PART ONE

THE MIRROR AND THE SPLINTERS

L ISTEN! This is the beginning. And when we get to the end, we shall know more than we do now.

Once there was a wicked demon – one of the worst: it was the Devil. He was very pleased with himself because he had made a mirror that had a strange power. Anything good and beautiful reflected in it shrunk away, while everything bad and ugly swelled up. The loveliest countryside looked like boiled spinach; the prettiest people looked horrible, and seemed to be standing on their heads or to have no stomachs at all. As for faces, the mirror twisted them so that you couldn't even recognize yourself. One single freckle would turn into a great blotch over your nose and your mouth. That's the Devil's idea of a joke!

If a good thought went through anyone's mind while he was looking in the mirror, it pulled a face at him. The Devil had a good laugh at that, too. All the pupils at his school for demons said it was a miracle.

This is the real world, they said; this mirror shows what people are really like. And they ran around with it until there wasn't anyone or any place that hadn't been twisted by it.

Then the demons wanted to fly up to heaven, to make fun of the angels and even of God himself. The higher they flew, the more the mirror grinned like a gargoyle. They could scarcely hold it still. The mirror shook and grinned, and grinned and shook, till they dropped it, and it fell straight down here to earth and broke into a million billion splinters.

That was only the start of the trouble. Some of the splinters were scarcely the size of a grain of sand, and they blew everywhere, getting into people's eyes and making them see everything ugly and twisted. Some splinters even got into people's hearts, and that was awful, because their hearts became like blocks of ice.

Some of the pieces of glass were big enough to use as windowpanes, but it didn't do to look at your friends through that sort of window. Others were made into spectacles, and the people who wore them never could see things straight. The Devil laughed so much he nearly split his sides. And he's laughing still, because there are plenty of those splinters flying about right now, as you will hear.

PART TWO

A LITTLE BOY AND A LITTLE GIRL

IN the city there are so many houses, not everyone can have a garden. Most people make do with a few flowers in a flowerpot. But once there were two children who did have a garden a bit bigger than a flowerpot. They weren't brother and sister, but they loved each other just as if they were. Their families lived next door to each other, right up in the attics. Where the roofs joined, they each had a little window, face to face, and you only had to clamber over the gutter to get from one window to the other.

Their fathers each put a wooden box across this gutter, to grow herbs for the kitchen. There were little rose trees, too, one in each box, that grew like anything. What with sweet peas trailing over the sides of the boxes and the rose trees twining their branches over the windows, the little garden was just perfect. Of course, as it was so high up, the children weren't allowed to climb on the boxes, but they often went out to sit under the roses and play together.

In winter these games had to stop. The windows were all iced up. But if you warmed a coin on the stove and put it to the frozen pane, it made a round peephole, and behind each peephole was a friendly eye of a little boy or a little girl. He was Kay and she was Gerda. In summer they could meet with one jump, but in winter they had to climb down a lot of stairs and then climb up a lot of stairs, and all the time the snowflakes were falling outside.

"Those are the white bees swarming," said the little girl's old grandmother.

"Have they got a queen?" asked the boy, because he knew that real bees have one.

"Yes, they have," said the grandmother. "She flies at the heart of the swarm. She's the biggest of them all. *She* never lies on the ground; she soars up again into the dark cloud. Many's the winter night she flies through the streets of this very town and spies through the windows, making them freeze over with patterns like flowers."

"I've seen that," cried both the children, and so they knew it was true.

"Could the Snow Queen come in here?" asked the little girl.

"Just let her try!" said the boy. "I'd put her on the hot stove and melt her."

But the grandmother stroked his hair and went on to other stories.

In the evening, when little Kay was back at home and nearly ready for bed, he climbed onto the stool by the window and peeped out through the little hole. A few snowflakes were sifting down, and one of these, the biggest of them all, rested on the edge of the windowbox outside. This snowflake grew and grew until it became a lady dressed in the finest white gossamer, made of millions of starry flakes. She was so delicate and beautiful – but she was ice, dazzling, glittering ice. Yet she was alive. Her eyes burned like stars, and there was neither peace nor rest in them. She nodded at the window and beckoned with her hand. The little boy was scared and jumped down from his stool. Outside he fancied he saw a huge bird swoop past the window.

Next day there was a clear frost. Then there was a thaw, and then it was spring. The sun shone and the trees budded green. The swallows built their nests, and the windows were opened wide so that the children could sit once more in their little garden high above the houses.

How wonderful the roses were that summer! They were more beautiful than ever. Gerda had learned a hymn that made her think of her roses, and she sang it to Kay, and he sang along:

When Jesus Christ
Was yet a child
He had a garden
Fair and wild.

And that's how it felt to them in those glorious summer days, as they sat holding hands among the roses, in God's own golden sunshine.

One day Kay and Gerda were looking at a picture book full of animals and birds, when suddenly – just as the clock struck five in the old church tower – Kay cried, "Oh! What's that pain in my heart? And, oh! What's that in my eye?"

The little girl put her arm around his neck, and he blinked his eye, but there was nothing to be seen.

"It must have gone," he said, but it had not gone. It was one of those splinters of glass from the mirror – you remember, the Devil's mirror, the one that made anything good look ugly and small and anything bad look fine and grand. Poor Kay! He had a splinter in his heart, too, which would turn it into a block of ice. It didn't hurt anymore, but it was there all right.

"What are you bawling about?" he asked. "You look so ugly! There's nothing wrong with me." Then, "Ugh! That rose is all wormy! And that one's all bent! What horrible roses!" He kicked the windowbox and tore off the rose blooms.

"Kay, what are you doing?" cried the little girl. When he saw how frightened she was, he pulled off another rose and ran away from his friend Gerda, back through the window.

After that, when Gerda brought out the picture book, he scoffed and said it was for babies. And when the grandmother told them stories now, he interrupted all the time and kept saying, "But . . ." Sometimes he would get behind her and put on her spare glasses and make fun of her. He really was like her, so people had to laugh.

Soon he could mimic everyone in the street, and he was especially good at anything that was odd or nasty. People said, "He's so sharp he'll cut himself!" It was the splinter in his eye and the splinter in his heart that had changed him and made him tease even little Gerda, who loved him more than all the world.

He never wanted to play now, he just made experiments. For instance, one winter's day when it was snowing, he brought out a big magnifying glass and then held out the tail of his blue jacket to catch some flakes. "Look through the glass, Gerda," he said. And she saw that the flakes looked much bigger, and each one was like a lovely flower or a six-pointed star. It was beautiful.

"Isn't that clever?" said Kay. "So much nicer than real flowers. They're just perfect – until they melt."

Later Kay came around with his big gloves on and his sled on his back. He shouted right in Gerda's ear, "They're letting me go and sled in the square with the other boys," and off he went.

Out in the square the boldest boys were tying their sleds to the farmers' carts to hitch a ride. It was great fun. As they were playing, a great big sleigh drew up. It was painted white all over, and in it was a figure muffled up in white fur, with a white fur cap, This sleigh drove twice around the square, and Kay, quick as anything, tied his sled behind it. The big sleigh went fast and then faster still and turned off into the main street. The driver turned and gave Kay a nod, as if they

were old friends. And every time Kay thought of untying his sled, the stranger nodded again, so Kay stayed where he was. They drove right out of the city gates.

Then it began to snow so heavily that the little boy could barely see his hand in front of his face, but still the great sleigh rushed on and on. And even when he did manage to untie the rope, it was no use. His little toboggan clung fast to the big sleigh, as they sped on with the wind at their tail. He called out at the top of his voice, but no one could hear him. The snow kept falling, and the sleigh drove on. Now and then it seemed to give a little jump as if it were leaping over hedges and ditches. Kay was filled with terror, and he tried to say the Lord's Prayer – but all he could remember was the twelve-times table.

The snowflakes were getting bigger and bigger, until they looked like great white birds. Then suddenly they swerved aside, the big sleigh stopped, and its driver stood up, in a fur cloak and a cap made of thick, thick snow. It was a lady – tall and slender and dazzlingly white. It was the Snow Queen.

"We have come far," she said. "But why do you tremble? Come, creep under my fur." And she put Kay beside her in her sleigh and wrapped the fur around him. Kay felt as if he were sinking into a deep drift of snow.

"Are you still frozen?" she asked, and she kissed him on the forehead. Oh! Her kiss was colder than cold. It went straight to his heart, which was nearly a lump of ice anyway. He thought he would die – but only for a moment. Then everything was all right, and he didn't feel cold anymore.

"My sled! Don't forget my sled!" That was his first thought. So it was tied to one of the white birds, which flew behind them with the little sled at its back. Then the Snow Queen kissed Kay once more, and he forgot little Gerda, and her grandmother, and everyone at home.

"No more kisses now," she said, "or I'll kiss you to death."

Kay gazed at her. She was so beautiful, more beautiful than he could grasp. Now she didn't seem to be made of ice, as she had been when she beckoned him at the window. He thought she was perfect, and he was not afraid. He told her he could do mental arithmetic – with fractions, too! – and that he knew exactly how many square miles there were in the country and how many people lived in it. But she just smiled, till it seemed to him that he really didn't know anything at all. Then he looked up into the huge, huge sky, and they rose up into it, up above the storm clouds, while the winds whistled snatches of sad old songs into their ears. They flew over forests, they flew over lakes, they flew over sea and land, while below them howled the icy blast and above them wheeled the black, screaming crows. Wolves cried, the snow glittered. Rising above everything, the great clear moon shone in Kay's eyes the length of the long, long winter night. And come day, he slept at the feet of the Snow Queen.

PART THREE

THE OLD WOMAN'S FLOWER GARDEN

BUT what did little Gerda think when Kay didn't come back? Where could he be? Nobody knew; nobody could tell her. All the boys could say was that they had seen him tie his little sled to a big one, which drove off down the street and through the city gate. Nobody knew what had become of him. Oh, the grief! Little Gerda wept bitter tears. People said Kay must be dead – drowned in the river that flowed past the city. It was a long, dark winter.

But at last the spring came, and the warm sunshine.

"Kay is dead and gone," said little Gerda.

"I don't believe it!" said the sunshine.

"He is dead and gone," she said to the swallows.

"We don't believe it!" they said. And after that, Gerda didn't believe it either.

"I will put on my new red shoes," she said one morning, "the ones Kay has never seen, and I'll go down to the river and ask for him."

It was still early. Gerda kissed her grandmother as she lay asleep and set off through the town gate to the river.

"Have you really taken my friend?" she asked. "I'll give you my red shoes if you'll give him back again."

It did seem as if the rippling water nodded to her, so she took off her precious red shoes and threw them into the river. But they fell close to the bank, and the little waves brought them straight back to her. It was as if the river didn't want her dearest possession, because it didn't have Kay. Or perhaps she hadn't thrown them far enough. So she clambered into a boat that was drawn up in the reeds, went right to the far end, and threw the shoes into the water once more. But the boat wasn't tied up, and her motion made it push off from the bank. Before she could move, it was yards out and drifting faster all the time.

Little Gerda was frightened and began to cry. But only the sparrows heard her, and they couldn't fetch her back to dry land. Instead they flew along the bank, singing as if to comfort her, "Here we are! Here we are!" Down the stream went the boat, faster and faster, while Gerda sat quite still in her stockinged feet. Her little red shoes bobbed along behind, but they couldn't catch up.

The riverbanks were beautiful. There were lovely flowers, ancient trees, and meadows dotted with sheep and cows, but there wasn't a

single human being. "Perhaps the river is taking me to Kay," thought Gerda, and that cheered her up. She stood up to get a better look at the beautiful green banks.

At last she came to a cherry orchard, where there was a little thatched house with funny blue and red windows and two wooden soldiers standing guard outside, presenting arms to anyone who passed. Gerda thought they were alive and called out to them, but of course they didn't answer. Then the river took her even closer, and she called again, louder, and out of the house came an old, old woman leaning on a shepherd's crook. She was wearing a big sunhat, painted all over with beautiful flowers.

"You poor little thing," said the old woman. "Whatever takes you on this big rushing river, floating out into the wide, wide world?" And with her crook she pulled the boat to the bank, and she lifted little Gerda out. Gerda was so pleased to be back on dry land, though she was just the least bit scared of the strange old woman.

"Now tell me all about yourself," the old woman said, "who you are, and how you got here."

So Gerda told her everything, and the old woman kept shaking her head and going, "*Hmmm. hmmm!*" till Gerda was finished. When Gerda asked her if she had seen Kay, the old woman said he hadn't come that way, but not to worry, for he was sure to do so. "Don't fret! Come and taste my cherries, and look at my lovely flowers. They're prettier than any picture book and can tell a better story, too." She took Gerda by the hand, and they went into the little house, and the old woman locked the door.

The windows were all high up, and the glass in them was red, blue, and yellow, so the daylight shone through them strangely. But there were the most delicious cherries on the table, and Gerda was allowed to eat as many as she liked. While she ate them, the old woman combed Gerda's hair with a golden comb till her curls shone like gold around her rosy little face.

"I've longed for a dear little girl just like you," the old woman said. "You'll see how happy we shall be." And the more she combed Gerda's hair, the more the little girl forgot about Kay. For the old woman could work magic, though she wasn't a witch; she just made spells for her own pleasure, and she wanted to keep Gerda for herself. So now she went into the garden and made all the roses hide under the dark earth so that you couldn't see where they had been. She was afraid the roses would remind Gerda of Kay, and then she might run away.

Now she showed Gerda the flower garden. It was such a perfect garden, you can't imagine. The blooms! The scents! Every plant you can think of, from every season of the year, all in flower at the same time. They were better than any picture book. Gerda played in the garden until the sun sank behind the cherry trees. Then she was given a lovely bed with red silk pillows stuffed with violets. She slept as happy as a queen on her wedding night.

On the next day and for many days she played among the flowers in the bright sunshine. Soon she knew every flower, and although there were so many, she couldn't help feeling that one was missing – which one, she couldn't say. Then one day she was sitting looking at the old woman's sunhat with the flowers painted on it, and she saw that the prettiest of all was a rose. The old woman had forgotten that one when she magicked the others underground. That's what happens if you don't keep your wits about you.

"Oh!" said Gerda. "Why are there no roses here?" And she ran from flowerbed to flowerbed, searching, searching, but she couldn't find a single one. Then she sat down and cried, and her warm tears fell just where a rose had buried itself, making the rose spring up as full of flowers as before. Gerda put her arms around it, and kissed the roses, and thought of the roses in the roof garden at home, and then she remembered Kay.

"What am I doing here?" she cried. "I ought to be looking for Kay!" She asked the roses, "Do you know where be is? Do you think he's dead and gone?"

"He is not dead," they replied. "We have been in the earth among the dead, and he was not there."

"Thank you," said little Gerda, and she went around to all the other flowers and looked into their cups and asked, "Do you know where Kay is?" But the flowers were just dozing in the sunshine, dreaming their own fairy tales. Gerda heard her fill of these, but none of them mentioned Kay.

What did the tiger lily say?

"Listen! The drums go *Boom! Boom!* Always the same notes: *Boom! Boom!* Listen to the wailing of the women! Listen to the chanting of the priests! The Hindu woman stands by the funeral pyre in her long red robe. The flames leap up around her and around her dead husband. But the woman is thinking of the living one in the circle, he whose eyes burn fiercer than fire, whose eyes consume her heart as the flames consume her body. Can the heart's flame ever be quenched?"

"I don't understand that at all," said Gerda.

"But that's my story," said the tiger lily.

What did the bindweed say?

"High above the narrow path hangs the old castle. The ivy is thick on the old stone walls, leaf after leaf twining up to the balcony where a beautiful girl is standing. She leans out and gazes down the path. No rose is fresher on the branch than she, no apple blossom more delicate as the wind spins it from the tree. Her silk gown rustles as she moves . . . 'When will he come?'"

"Is it Kay?" asked Gerda.

"I'm only telling my story," said the bindweed.

What did the tiny snowdrop say?

"The swing hangs on ropes between the trees. Two pretty girls, in frocks as white as snow, are swinging. Green silk ribbons are fluttering from their hats. Their brother is bigger than they. He stands on the swing with his arm round the rope to keep steady. In one hand he has a saucer, in the other a clay pipe. He is blowing bubbles. The soap bubbles drift, back and forth. The swing swings, back and forth, back and forth. The last bubble sways from the bowl of the pipe. A bubbly little black dog is on his hind legs trying to get on the swing. But it

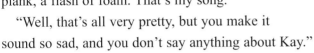

flies past, and
he falls down with
an angry yelp. The
children laugh, the
bubble bursts. A swinging
plank, a flash of foam. That's my song."

"Well, that's all very pretty, but you make it
sound so sad, and you don't say anything about Kay."

What did the hyacinths say?

"There were three lovely sisters, as fine as fine. The first
was dressed in red, the second in blue, the third in pure white. The
moon shone on them as they danced hand in hand by the still lake.
They were not fairies, but of human kind. The breeze blew sweet, and
the girls vanished into the forest. The breeze blew strong, and three
coffins, with the lovely maids lying in them, floated out from the dark
wood, over the lake. The fireflies hovered around them, like tiny
lamps. Are the dancing sisters dead, or do they sleep? The scent of the
flowers tells me they are dead. The bells toll for them."

"You make me feel so sad," said Gerda, "and your own scent is so
cloying, I can't help thinking of the dead girls. Can Kay be dead too?
The roses have been down underground, and they say he isn't."

"*Dong! Dong! Dong!*" tolled the hyacinth bells. "We're not ringing
for little Kay; we don't know him. We're just singing our song. It's the
only one we know."

The buttercup shone bright among its green leaves. "Bright little
sun," pleaded Gerda, "tell me where I can find my friend."

The buttercup beamed. But what song did it sing? Nothing about
Kay.

"In the small backyard the sun was shining. It was the first day of spring, and the sunbeams slid down the whitewashed wall. The first yellow flowers were showing, gleaming gold in the warm sunshine. The old grandmother was sitting outside, and her granddaughter, a poor, pretty servant girl, who was home on a visit, kissed her. There was pure heart's gold in the blessing of that kiss. And that's my story," said the buttercup.

"My poor old grandmother," said Gerda. "She must be missing me, and Kay too! But I'll be home soon, bringing Kay with me. It's no use asking these flowers. They only know their own songs and can't tell me anything."

She hitched up her skirt so that she could run faster, but the narcissus caught at her leg, so she stopped to ask, "Do you know anything?" What did it say?

"I can see myself! I can see myself! Ah! How sweet my scent is! Up in the attic, I see a little dancer. First she stands on one foot, then the other, and then she aims her high kicks at the whole world. But of course it's all in the mind. She is pouring water from a teapot onto a bit of stuff she's holding. It's her bodice. Well, cleanliness is next to godliness. Her white dress is hanging from a peg. She's washed that in the teapot, too, and hung it up to dry. Now she's putting it on, with a yellow scarf. That makes the dress even whiter. Up goes her leg! How she struts on just one stalk. I can see myself! I can see myself!"

"I can't stand around listening to this," said Gerda. "It's no use to me." She ran to the end of the garden. The gate was locked, but she shook it till the rusty bolt gave way and the door flew open. Little Gerda ran out barefoot into the wide world. She looked back three times, but nobody followed.

When she couldn't run anymore, she sat down on a big stone. She looked around. Summer was gone; it was late autumn. You couldn't tell in the garden because the sun always shone there and the flowers of all the seasons were always in bloom.

"I have tarried too long," said little Gerda. "Autumn has come. I must go on." And she limped off.

How tired and sore her feet were. Everything was so bleak and cold. The long willow leaves were all yellow and damp with dew. One by one they fell. Only the sloe still kept its fruit, and that was so bitter it made you wince. Oh, how mournful and grey it was in the wide world!

PART FOUR

A PRINCE AND A PRINCESS

GERDA had to rest again. Hopping about in the snow just by her was a great big crow, who looked at her for a long time before he nodded his head and said, "*Caw! Caw!* Hallaw! Hallaw!" That was the best he could manage at human speech. He liked the look of the little girl and asked her where she was heading, all alone in the wide world. "Alone" – Gerda knew all too well what that word meant. She told the crow all about herself and asked if he hadn't seen Kay.

The crow nodded gravely and said, "Cawed be! Cawed bel"

"Oh! Do you really think so?" cried the little girl, and she hugged the bird so tightly she nearly throttled him.

"Wawtch out! Wawtch out!" said the crow. "lt might have been he. But if it was, he's forsaken you for a princess."

"Is he living with a princess?" asked Gerda.

"Yes. Listen!" said the crow. "But your talk makes my poor throat hurt. If only you spoke Crow!"

"I've never learned it," said Gerda. "But my grandmother could speak it, and Gobbledegook, too."

"Never mind," said the crow. "I'll do my best." And this is what he tried to say.

"ln this kingdom there lives a princess who is so clever that she has read all the newspapers in the world. And what's more, she's forgotten them again, which just shows you how clever she is. Now, she was sitting on her throne the other day, at a bit of a loose end, when she started humming a song that went like this:

I'm getting tired of the single life,
It's about time I was a wife.
They can run but they can't hide,
I'll find the man to make me a bride.

"And she said, '*Hmmm*. There's something to be said for that.' So she decided she would get married, but only to a man who could speak when he was spoken to, not one who just stood around looking important – that would be even more boring. So she drummed up all her ladies-in-waiting, and when they heard what she planned, they were as pleased as pleased. 'What a good idea! We thought of it ourselves only the other day!' This is not a word of a lie," said the crow. "I got this from my sweetheart, who is tame and has the run of the palace." Of course the sweetheart was a crow too; birds of a feather flock together, as they say.

"The next day's newspapers were printed up with a border of hearts and the princess's initials. And inside they said that any good-looking young man was free to come up to the palace and meet the princess. And the one who could chat away as if he were at home would win her. Take it from me, it's true! Well, come one, come all; there were crowds of them. But none of them was up to scratch. Out in the street they all had the gift of the gab, but once inside the palace gates, under the eye of the guards in their silver uniforms and the footmen in gold, they lost their tongues. And when they stood in the glittering throne room and the princess spoke to them, they couldn't do anything but parrot the last thing she said, and she didn't need to hear that again. It was as if they'd taken something to make them sleepy, and they didn't wake up till they got outside again. They could talk nineteen to the

dozen then! There was a line all the way from the town gates to the palace. They were hungry and thirsty, and they didn't get so much as a glass of water from the palace. The sensible ones had brought sandwiches with them, but they wouldn't share them with the others. They thought, 'The princess won't waste her time on starvelings.'"

"But Kay, little Kay!" said Gerda. "When did he come? Was he in the crowd?"

"Give me a chance! Give me a chance! I'm just getting to him. On the third day a perky little chap marches up to the palace without a horse or a carriage. His eyes were bright like yours, and he had lovely flowing hair, but his clothes were in a right state – quite shabby."

"That was Kay!" cried Gerda. "I've found him at last!" And she clapped her hands.

"He had a little knapsack on his back," said the crow.

"That must have been his sled," said Gerda. "He had that with him."

"Maybe," said the crow. "I didn't look too closely. But my sweetheart told me that when he walked through the palace gates and saw the sentries in silver and the footmen in gold, he wasn't the least put out. He just nods at them and says, 'It must be very boring standing around on the stairs all day. I'd sooner go inside!' And even though the rooms were glittering with lights, and important-looking folk were tiptoeing about with golden dishes, he wasn't outfaced. His boots squeaked like anything, but he wasn't worried."

"That's my Kay," said Gerda. "He had new boots; I heard them squeak in Grandmother's kitchen."

"Yes, they squeaked all right," said the crow, "but he went cheerfully up to the princess, who was sitting on a pearl as big as a spinning wheel. All the ladies-in-waiting with their maids and their

maids' maids, and all the courtiers with their footmen and their footmen's footmen, were ranged about, and the nearer they were to the door the prouder they looked. The palace bootboy was standing in the door, and he was so proud you daren't look at him!"

"Oh how awful!" said Gerda. "And Kay still won the princess?"

"If I wasn't a crow I'd have had a go myself, even though I am engaged. My sweetheart said he spoke as well as I do when I'm speaking Crow. He was witty and charming; he hadn't come to woo the princess but just to hear her talk – she was so wise! And she liked him."

"It must have been Kay!" said Gerda. "He's so clever, he can do mental arithmetic, with fractions! Oh, take me to him."

"That's more easily said than done," said the crow. "But I'll talk to my sweetheart, and she'll know what to do. All I know is, a girl like you wouldn't be let in in the normal run of things."

"I would," said Gerda. "As soon as Kay heard it was me; he'd come straight out to fetch me."

"Well, just wait for me by that stile," said the crow, wagging his head, and off he flew.

It was late afternoon when the crow came back again. "*Caw! Caw!*" he said. "My sweetheart sends her best wishes, and this crust of bread from the kitchen; they won't miss it, and you must be hungry. It's out of the question for you to go to the palace barefoot as you are; the guards in silver and the footmen in gold won't stand for it. But don't fret, you'll still get in. My sweetheart knows a little back staircase that leads up to the bedchamber, and she knows where the key is kept."

So they went into the garden and along the wide avenue where the leaves were falling, one by one, and as the palace lights went out, one by one, the crow brought little Gerda to a back door that was open just a crack.

Oh, how Gerda's heart was beating with fear and longing! She felt she was doing wrong, yet all she wanted was to see if Kay was there. Surely it must be he. In her mind's eye she could see his bright eyes and his long hair. She could just picture him back home, smiling among the roses. He would be glad to see her, and to hear how far she had come for his sake and how much they all missed him at home. She was so happy, and so afraid.

Now they were on the stairs. A little lamp was burning on a stand, and the tame crow was waiting for them. Gerda curtseyed, as her grandmother had taught her.

"My fiancé has told me a lot of nice things about you, my dear," said the tame crow. "The fairy tale of your life, if I may call it so, touches the heart. If you take the lamp, I will lead the way. If we go straight we'll not meet anyone."

"But someone is following us," said Gerda. Something rushed past her: shadows on the wall, horses with flowing manes and slender legs, huntsmen, lords and ladies on horseback.

"Those are but dreams," said the tame crow. "They fetch the gentry's thoughts to the midnight hunt. And that's just as well, for you'll be able to look more closely while they sleep. All I can say is, when you come into fame and fortune, don't forget us."

"There's no need for that" said the crow from the forest.

Now they came into the first room. The walls were hung with rose-red satin, embroidered with flowers. Here the dreams were rushing past so swiftly that Gerda could not make them out. Each new room was more sumptuous than the last; it made her quite dizzy. And now they

were in the royal bedchamber. The ceiling was like a huge palm tree with leaves of crystal, and in the middle of the room there were two beds shaped like lilies, hanging from a golden stalk. One of them was white, and that was where the princess was lying. The other was red, and that was where Gerda looked for Kay. She bent back a red petal and saw a brown neck. It was Kay! She cried his name aloud, holding the lamp over his face. His dreams whirled back to him. He awoke, he turned his head, and – no! It wasn't Kay.

It was only the neck that looked like Kay's, though the prince, too, was young and handsome. The princess woke up in her lily bed and asked what was happening. Little Gerda burst into tears and told her whole story, with everything that the crows had done for her.

"You poor little thing," said the prince and princess. They praised the crows and weren't angry at all, this once. The crows would even get a reward.

"Would you like to fly away free," asked the princess, "or would you like to be appointed Crows to the Court, with a right to all the kitchen scraps?

Both the crows bowed and said they would like the official appointment, as they had to think of their old age, and "you want something put by for a rainy day."

Then the prince got out of his bed and put Gerda to sleep in it. He couldn't do more than that. She folded her hands and thought, "How kind everyone is – animals and people." She closed her eyes and went to sleep. The dreams all came back again, and they looked just like angels, pulling a little sled with Kay on it, nodding at her – but it was just a dream, gone as soon as she woke.

The next day the prince and princess dressed her from top to toe in silk and velvet. They invited her to stay at the palace and join in the fun. But all she wanted was a little horse and carriage and a pair of boots so she could drive out once more into the wide world to look for Kay.

They gave her the boots and a muff as well. And when she was all dressed up in her beautiful new clothes, a carriage of pure gold drew up at the door, with the coats of arms of the prince and princess glittering on it like stars. The coachmen, the footmen, and the outriders – yes, she even had outriders – had gold crowns on their heads. The prince and princess themselves helped her into the carriage and wished her good luck, and the forest crow, who was married now, saw her on her way for the first few miles. He sat beside her in the carriage. The tame crow stayed behind in the gateway, flapping her wings. All those kitchen scraps had given her a headache. Inside, the carriage was lined with sugar candy, and underneath the seat were ginger nuts.

"Goodbye! Goodbye!" cried the prince and princess. Little Gerda wept, and so did the crow. They went on like that for three miles, and then the crow said "Goodbye!" too, and that was the hardest parting of them all. He flew up into a tree and flapped his gleaming wings as long as he could see the carriage, which shone back at him like bright, bright sunshine.

PART FIVE

THE LITTLE ROBBER GIRL

O N they drove through the dark forest. The carriage shone so fiercely it dazzled the robber band.

"It's gold! It's gold!" they cried. They rushed out, seized the horses, killed the coachman and the footmen and the outriders, and dragged little Gerda from the coach.

"She's plump; she's a dainty morsel; she's been fattened on nuts!" said the old robber woman, who had a bristly beard and shaggy eyebrows. "She's a tasty lambkin. She makes my mouth water." And she drew her bright knife, which glittered menacingly.

"Ouch!" screeched the old hag all of a sudden. She had been bitten in the ear by her own fierce daughter, who was clinging to her back. "You vile brat!" said her mother, quite forgetting to kill Gerda.

"She can play with me," said the little robber girl. "She shall give me her muff and her pretty dress and sleep in my bed." And she bit her mother again, so that the robber woman leaped right round in the air and the other robbers laughed at her, shouting, "Look at the tigress dancing with her cub!"

"I want to go in the carriage," said the little robber girl. She always got her own way, she was so spoiled and stubborn. So she and Gerda sat inside while they rattled over bushes and briars through the forest. The little robber girl was the same height as Gerda but broader, stronger, and darker-skinned. Her eyes were quite black, with an odd, sad look. She put her arm round Gerda's waist and said, "They won't kill you, as long as I'm not cross with you. Are you a princess?"

"No," said Gerda. "I'm not a princess." And she told her everything that had happened, and how much she loved Kay.

The robber girl listened solemnly and said, "I won't let them kill you, even if I do get angry. I'll do it myself!" Then she dried Gerda's eyes and wrapped her hands in the warm muff.

The carriage pulled up in the courtyard of the robbers' castle. There were cracks right up the walls; crows and ravens were flying in and out of holes; great bulldogs, which looked as if they could gulp down a man, were leaping about, though they weren't allowed to bark. A huge fire was burning on the stone floor of the old hall, hung with cobwebs and soot; soup was simmering in a massive cauldron, and hares and rabbits were roasting on the spit.

"Tonight you'll sleep with me and my pets," said the robber girl. They had something to eat and drink and then made their way to a corner where there was straw and some blankets. About a hundred pigeons, asleep on their high perches, ruffled themselves when the girls arrived, "They're all mine," said the little robber girl, and she grabbed the nearest one by its legs and shook it till its wings flapped. "Give it a kiss!" she cried, shoving it in Gerda's face.

Then she pointed to some wooden slats nailed over a hole above their heads. "Those two wood pigeons in there are forest riffraff. They'd fly off if you didn't keep them locked up." Then she pulled a reindeer forward by its antlers; it was tethered and had a bright copper ring round its neck. "This is my old love, Bae! I've got to keep him tied up, too, or he'd be up and off. Every night I have to tickle his neck with my dagger, just to put some fear in him!" And the little girl drew a long knife from a crack in the wall and slid it across the reindeer's neck. The poor beast kicked out, and the robber girl chuckled and pulled Gerda down into her bed.

"Do you keep your knife with you while you sleep?" asked Gerda, looking at it nervously.

"I always sleep with a knife by me," said the little robber girl. "You never know what will happen. But now tell me again about little Kay, and why you've come out into the wide world." So Gerda told her tale once more, from the very beginning, while the wood pigeons murmured in their cage and the other pigeons slept. The little robber girl put her arm round Gerda's neck, with her knife in the other hand. She fell asleep – you could hear that – but Gerda couldn't close her eyes for a moment, not knowing if she was to live or die. The robbers sat round the fire, drinking and singing, while the old robber woman turned somersaults. Little Gerda was filled with dread.

Then the wood pigeons said, "*Coo! Coo!* We've seen little Kay. A white bird was carrying his sled, and he was sitting in the Snow Queen's carriage, which flew low over the forest as we lay in our nest. She breathed on the young ones and all of them died except us two. *Coo! Coo!*"

"What's that?" asked Gerda. "Where was the Snow Queen going? Can you tell me?"

"She was probably going to Lapland, to the everlasting ice and snow. Ask the reindeer who's tied up over there."

"Yes," said the reindeer, "there's ice and snow in Lapland. It's wonderful! You can run free across the great shining valleys. That's where the Snow Queen has her summer tent. But her palace is up by the North Pole."

"Oh, Kay! Poor Kay!" said Gerda with a sigh.

"Lie still!" said the robber girl. "If you don't want a knife in your belly!"

When morning came, Gerda told her everything the wood pigeons had said, and the little robber girl looked at her solemnly and said, "Never mind. Never mind." Then she asked the reindeer, "Do you know where Lapland is?"

"Who better than I?" he answered, his eyes alight. "I was born there and I was bred there, running free across the fields of snow."

"Listen," said the robber girl to Gerda. "All the men have gone out, but my ma's still here, and she'll stick around. Later in the morning she'll have a swig from that big bottle, and after that she'll have a snooze. Then I'll see what I can do for you." She jumped out of bed, threw her arms round her mother's neck, pulled her beard, and said, "Morning, you old nannygoat!" And her mother gave her a punch on the nose that turned it red and blue – just as a token of affection.

When the old woman had swigged her drink and dropped off into her snooze, the robber girl went to the reindeer and said, "I'd like to tickle your throat some more with my knife because it makes me laugh, but never mind. I'm going to let you off your rope and set you free so that you can go to Lapland. But you must put your best foot foremost and carry this little girl to the Snow Queen's palace for me. That's where her playmate is; but you'll have heard that, because she wasn't quiet about it and you were listening!"

The reindeer jumped for joy. The robber girl lifted Gerda onto his back and carefully tied her on, with a little cushion for comfort. "You'll be all right," she said. "You can have your fur boots, because it's getting cold, but I'm keeping your muff, because it's so pretty. You won't freeze. You can have my ma's big gloves. They'll reach right up

to your elbows. Put your paws in! Now they look just like my ugly old ma's!"

Gerda wept with happiness.

"I can't abide that grizzling," said the little robber girl. "You ought to be pleased. Anyway, here are two loaves and a ham, so you won't starve." She tied these on the reindeer. Then she opened the door, called in the dogs, cut the rope, and said to the reindeer, "Off you go! Take care of the little girl!"

Gerda stretched out her hands in the huge gloves and said goodbye to the robber girl, and then the reindeer leapt away over bush and briar, through the great forest, over marsh and moor, as fast as he could go. Wolves howled; ravens shrieked; the wind whistled past, *shioo, shioo.* The sky flashed red as if the world were sneezing.

"Those are my dear old Northern Lights," said the reindeer. "Putting on their show!" And he ran on faster than ever, through the night, through the day. The loaves were eaten. The ham was eaten. They were in Lapland.

PART SIX

THE LAPP WOMAN
AND THE FINN WOMAN

T HEY stopped at a ramshackle little hut. The roof came right down to the ground, and the door was so low that the family had to crawl on all fours to get in or out. There was no one at home except an old Lapp woman, who was cooking fish over an oil lamp. The reindeer told her Gerda's story, though first he told his own, which seemed much more important. Gerda was too bone-cold to speak.

"Oh you poor things!" said the Lapp woman. "You've still a long way to go! It's over a hundred miles to Finmark, and that's where you'll find the Snow Queen. She's staying in the country there, setting off her fireworks every night. I'll scribble a note on a piece of dried cod – I haven't any paper – and you can take that to the Finn woman up there. She can give you better directions than I."

When Gerda was warm again and had had something to eat and drink, the Lapp woman scribbled her note on a piece of dried cod, telling Gerda to take good care of it, then tied her securely on the reindeer's back, and off he went. *Shioo! Shioo!* went the wind, and up in the sky the Northern Lights burned blue and beautiful through the night.

And so they came to Finmark and knocked at the chimney of the Finn woman's house, as she didn't have a door.

Inside it was sweltering. The Finn woman herself barely had a stitch on. She was very dumpy and rather dirty. The first thing she did was loosen little Gerda's clothes and take off her gloves and boots; otherwise it would have been far too hot for her. She put a hunk of ice on the reindeer's head, and then read what was written on the cod. She read it three times, and when she had it by heart she dropped the cod into the cooking pot, because it was a tasty bit and she didn't like waste.

Now the reindeer told his story, and then little Gerda's, and the Finn woman blinked her wise eyes but said nothing.

"You know so much," said the reindeer. "You can bind the winds of the world with a thread of cotton. When the sailor unties the first knot, he gets a strong wind. If he unties the second, the wind begins to gust. If he ventures the third and fourth, he calls up a gale that will destroy a forest. Will you give the little girl a drink so that she'll have the strength of twelve to overcome the Snow Queen?"

"'The strength of twelve!'" said the Finn woman. "Much good that would do!" She went over to a shelf, took down a rolled-up parchment, and unrolled it. Strange characters were written on it; the Finn woman read till the sweat poured from her brow.

The reindeer begged so hard for little Gerda, and Gerda looked at her with such tearful, beseeching eyes, that the Finn woman began to blink her own eyes. She took the reindeer into a corner, and put more ice on his head, and whispered, "Little Kay is with the Snow Queen, right enough, and he's glad of it. He thinks he's in the best place in the world, because he's got a splinter of glass in his heart and a speck of glass in his eye. Unless you get them out, he'll never be human again, but will remain under the Snow Queen's sway."

"Can't you give Gerda something that will give her power?"

"I can't give her any more power than she has within her. Don't you feel how strong that is? Humans and beasts are at her service as she makes her way through the wide world on her two bare feet. But she must not learn of her power from us. It comes from the innocence of her dear child's heart. If she can't find her own way into the Snow Queen's palace and free little Kay by herself, there's nothing we can do to help. The Snow Queen's garden begins two miles on. Take her there, and put her down by the big bush with the red berries that stands out against the snow. Don't waste any time on idle chatter, but come back here as quick as you can." And with that the Finn woman lifted little Gerda onto the reindeer's back, and off he ran.

"Oh! I haven't got my boots! I haven't got my gloves!" shouted little Gerda as the cold started to bite, but the reindeer didn't dare stop. He ran till he came to the big bush with the red berries, and there he sat Gerda down and gave her a kiss, with big shining tears trickling down his face. Then he ran back swiftly, leaving poor Gerda standing without boots, without gloves, in the icy middle of freezing Finmark.

She ran forward as best she could, and a whole regiment of snowflakes appeared beside her. They weren't falling from the sky, which was clear and lit up by the Northern Lights. They were running along the ground, and the closer they came the bigger they grew. Gerda was reminded how strange and cleverly made the flakes had seemed when she saw them through the magnifying glass. Now they were even bigger and much more frightening. They were alive! They were the Snow Queen's border guards. They took weird shapes: some were like great ugly hedgehogs; some were like knots of writhing snakes; others were like stumpy little bears with icicle fur. They were all living white snowflakes.

Then Gerda began to say the Lord's Prayer. The cold was so bitter she could see her own breath coming from her mouth like smoke. The clouds of smoke grew thicker and thicker, and turned into little shining angels, who got bigger and bigger when they touched the ground. They had helmets and shields and spears. By the time Gerda had finished her prayer, she was surrounded by a whole army of them. They thrust their spears into the terrible snow creatures and shattered them into a thousand pieces, so that Gerda could go forward without fear. The angels rubbed her hands and feet, and at once she felt less cold. She hurried on toward the Snow Queen's palace.

But now let's see what Kay has been up to. He hasn't been thinking about Gerda, that's for sure. He never dreamed she was standing there outside the palace.

PART SEVEN

WHAT HAPPENED IN
THE SNOW QUEEN'S PALACE
AND WHAT HAPPENED AFTER THAT

T HE palace walls were of driven snow, and the doors and
windows were of biting wind. There were over a hundred
rooms, all made by the drifting snow. The biggest was miles
long. The whole vast, empty, glittering palace was lit by the Northern
Lights. It was icy. No revels were held there, not so much as a frolic
for the foxes or a dance for the polar bears, though the storm could
have made the music while the beasts walked on their hind legs and
performed their party pieces. Bare and cold was the palace of the Snow
Queen.

In the very middle was a frozen lake. It had split into a thousand
pieces, each piece exactly like every other. It was a miracle of science.
And in the middle of that lake the Snow Queen sat, when she was at
home. She called it the Mirror of Reason and said it was the only one
of its kind, and the best.

Little Kay was blue with cold. In fact he was almost black. But he
didn't notice, as the Snow Queen had kissed his shivers away and his
heart was just a lump of ice. He was dragging sharp, flat blocks of ice
here and there, as if he were trying to make them into patterns. And so
he was. They were the intricate patterns of the Puzzle of Reason and
Ice. To him these patterns seemed utterly important and remarkable;

that's because of the speck of glass in his eye. He was trying to join complete patterns to make a word, but somehow it wouldn't come out right. The word was ETERNITY. The Snow Queen had told him, "If you can work out that pattern for me, you will be your own master. I shall give you the whole world, and a new pair of skates." But he couldn't.

"I must be off to the warm countries," said the Snow Queen. "I'm going to have a peep into the black cauldrons, Etna and Vesuvius. I shall frost them over a bit. It's what they need, and good for the lemons and grapes." And away she flew, leaving Kay all alone in the vast ice halls, staring at the blocks of ice and thinking so hard you could hear him crack inside. There he sat, so stiff and still he might have frozen to death.

It was then that little Gerda stepped through the gate of wind into the palace. She said the Lord's Prayer, and the fierce winds lay down to sleep. She entered the vast, icy hall and saw Kay. She knew him at once and flung her arms tight round him, crying, "Kay! Dear Kay! I've found you at last!" But he sat quite still, stiff and cold.

Little Gerda wept: hot tears that fell upon his breast and sank right inside him. They melted the lump of ice and consumed the splinter of glass that was in his heart. Kay looked at Gerda, and then she sang the hymn they used to sing:

> *When Jesus Christ*
> *Was yet a child*
> *He had a garden*
> *Fair and wild.*

Then Kay burst into tears, and he cried away the splinter of glass that was in his eye. Then he recognized Gerda and shouted, "Gerda!

Dear Gerda! Where have you been for so long? And where have I been?" He looked about him. "Oh, it's so cold here! It's so vast and empty!" And he hugged Gerda to him, and they both laughed and cried for joy. The very blocks of ice danced with them, and when they were tired, the blocks laid themselves down in the pattern the Snow Queen had told Kay to work out, so that he should be his own master and have the whole world, and a new pair of skates.

Then Gerda kissed his cheeks and brought the bloom back to them; she kissed his eyes, and they shone like her own; she kissed his hands and feet, and he was safe and sound. The Snow Queen could come back whenever she liked; Kay's freedom was written plain on the shining ice.

Hand in hand they made their way out of the great palace, talking about Grandmother and the roses on the roof. Wherever they walked, the winds dropped away, and the sun shone. When they reached the bush with the red berries, the reindeer was waiting for them. With him was a young reindeer doe, who kissed the children and let them drink the warm milk from her full udders. Then the reindeer carried Kay and Gerda first to the Finn woman, to get warm in her hot room and learn how to get home, and then to the Lapp woman, who had new clothes and a sleigh ready for them.

The reindeer kept them company to the borders of their homeland, where the first green shoots were beginning to show. There Kay and Gerda said farewell to the reindeer and the Lapp woman. "Goodbye! Goodbye!" they all cried.

The small birds were twittering, and the woods were green with buds. And out of the woods there came a handsome horse. Gerda knew it – it was the horse that had pulled her gold carriage. And on it was a

girl with a bright red cap on her head and pistols at her side. It was the
little robber girl, who was fed up with home and heading north, or for
any other part that took her fancy. She and Gerda were very happy to
see each other.

"You're a fine fellow to go off on a spree," she said to Kay. "I
wonder if it was worth anyone's while running to the ends of the earth
for you."

But Gerda stroked her cheek and asked about the prince and
princess.

"They've gone off to foreign parts," said the robber girl.

"'And what about the crow?" asked Gerda.

"Oh the crow's dead," was the answer. "His tame sweetheart is a
widow now and wears a twist of black wool round her leg. She's such
a misery-guts; but it's all an act. But now you tell me your story, and
how you found him."

So Gerda and Kay told her the whole story.

"Ah well," said the robber girl. "Snip-snap-snout, your tale's told
out." Then she took them both by the hand and promised that if she
was ever passing through their town she would look them up. And then
she rode off into the wide world.

Kay and Gerda walked on hand in hand. As they went, the flowers
of spring blossomed about them. Church bells rang out, and they saw
the high towers of the city where they lived. They went to
Grandmother's door, up the staircase, and into the room. Everything
was just as it had been. The clock still said "*Tick tock*" as it always
had. But as they entered the room, they felt that they were not the
same. They had grown up.

The roses were flowering on the roof gutter, and near them were the

children's stools. Gerda and Kay sat down and held each other's hands. The Snow Queen's frozen, hollow majesty was forgotten like a bad dream. Grandmother sat with them in God's good sunshine, reading from the Bible: "Except ye become as little children, ye shall not enter the Kingdom of Heaven."

Kay and Gerda looked into each other's eyes, and now they understood the words of the hymn:

> *When Jesus Christ*
> *Was yet a child*
> *He had a garden*
> *Fair and wild.*

They were still children at heart. And where they sat it was summer: warm, blessed summer.

THE COLLAR

THERE was once a man-about-town whose only belongings were a bootjack and a comb. But he had the smartest shirt collar you ever saw, and it is the collar that this story is about.

The collar was about old enough to start thinking of taking a wife, when by chance he met a lady's garter in the wash.

"Oh!" gasped the collar. "You're the sweetest thing I've ever seen – so slim, so delicate, so pretty. What's your name?"

"I shan't tell you," snapped the garter.

"Where do you live?" asked the collar.

But the garter, who had a shrinking nature, thought this was a rather personal question, so she didn't answer.

"You must be some kind of undergarment," said the collar. "A girdle, perhaps. I can see that you must be as useful as you are decorative, my dear."

"How dare you talk to me like that!" said the garter. "I never gave you permission to."

"Beauty like yours gives its own permission," said the collar.

"Keep away!" squealed the garter. "You're too … masculine."

"It's true I am a man-about-town," said the collar. "I own a bootjack and a comb." But it wasn't true – he was just boasting. It was his master who owned the bootjack and the comb.

"Don't come so near!" the garter fluttered. "I'm not used to it!"

"Hoity-toity!" said the collar.

Then he was lifted out of the wash. He was starched, hung to dry over a chair in the sun, and laid on the ironing board, at the mercy of the hot iron.

"Madam," said the collar, "dear widow lady. You're getting me all hot. You're making a new man of me, you're smoothing out all my kinks. I feel I'm on fire. Oh! Be my wife!"

"Rag!" said the scornful iron, and she trundled back and forth over the collar, imagining she was a steam train. "Rag!"

The collar was a bit frayed at the edges, so the big scissors came along to trim the threads.

"Oh!" said the collar. "You must be a ballet dancer! Nobody could do the splits with more charm and grace."

"I know," said the scissors.

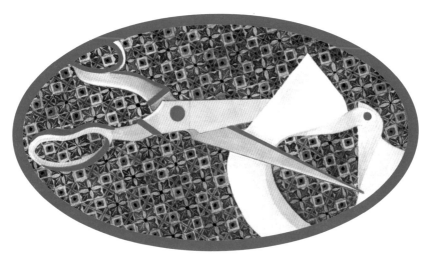

"You deserve to be a countess," said the collar. "All I can offer is a man-about-town, a bootjack, and a comb. If only I were a count!"

"The nerve!" said the scissors. "To propose to me!" And she gave him such a nasty cut that he would have to be thrown away.

There's nothing for it, I shall have to propose to the comb, thought the collar. "It's extraordinary, my dear," he said, "how you still have all your own teeth. Have you ever thought of getting married?"

"Didn't you know?" simpered the comb. "I'm engaged to the bootjack."

"Engaged!" said the collar.

Now there was no one left to propose to, which put him off the whole idea.

A long time passed, and then the collar found himself in the rag pile at the paper mill. There was quite a crowd of rags, but the fine ones kept their distance from the common ones, just like in life. They all had a lot to say, especially the collar, who was such a braggart.

"I had my pick of the girls," he said. "They just wouldn't leave me alone. I was a real man-about-town in those days – starched to the nines! My own bootjack and comb, which I never used! Those were the days! You should have seen me.

"I shall never forget my first love. She was a girdle – so delicate, so sweet, so pretty. She threw herself into a washtub for my sake.

"And then there was the widow. She really turned on the heat! But I snubbed her and it was her who got scorched.

"Then there was the ballet dancer. She had an artistic temperament; I still bear the scars to this day.

"My own comb was in love with me. I broke her heart, and all her teeth fell out.

"The stories I could tell! But I'm sorriest for the garter – I mean the girdle – who flung herself into the washtub. I've got a lot on my conscience. I deserve to be turned into blank paper."

And that is what happened. All the rags were pulped and made into blank paper, and the collar was made into this very page, with his own story printed on it. That's because he bragged so much afterwards about things that weren't true.

If we don't watch out, the same thing might happen to us. We'll end up in the rag pile, to be turned into blank paper and have our life story printed on it for the whole world to read – even the secret bits. Then we'll have to run around repeating it all, just like the collar.

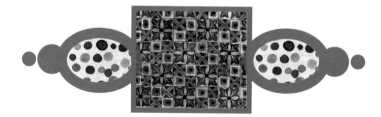

THE SHEPHERDESS
AND THE
CHIMNEY SWEEP

HAVE you ever seen a really old carved-wood cupboard, quite black with age? There was once one just like that in a sitting room; it had been in the family for generations. It was carved from top to bottom with roses and tulips, and little stags' heads with branching antlers peeping out from the twining leaves. And on the central panel was carved a funny man. He had a long beard, and little horns on his forehead, and the legs of a billygoat, and he had a grin on his face – you couldn't call it a smile. The children of the house called him "Brigadier-General Private Sergeant-Major Goatlegs," because it was hard to say, and there aren't many – living or carved – who can boast a title like that.

Anyhow, there he was. From the cabinet, he kept a close eye on the table under the mirror, because that was where the china shepherdess stood. She had golden shoes, and a golden hat, and a dress that was fetchingly pinned with a red rose. Oh, she was a picture!

Standing right next to her was a little chimney sweep; he too was made of china. Although he was as black as coal, you could tell he was only pretending to be a sweep. He was too neat and tidy, and his face was as pink and white as a girl's, without so much as a smut of soot on it. At the china works they might just as easily have made him into a prince as a chimney sweep.

Since the sweep and the shepherdess had always stood side by side on the table – he holding his ladder, and she her shepherd's crook – they naturally fell in love. They were a good match: two young people, both made of the same kind of porcelain, and each as fragile as the other.

Nearby there was another china figure, three times their size. It was an old Chinese Mandarin, who could nod his head, and who always claimed to be the shepherdess's grandfather. That made him her guardian, according to him, so when Brigadier-General Private Sergeant-Major Goatlegs asked for her hand in marriage, the old Mandarin nodded his consent.

"There's a husband for you," he said. "I am almost certain he is made of mahogany; and he will make you Lady Brigadier-General Private Sergeant-Major Goatlegs. He has a cupboard full of silver, and who knows what else."

"I don't want to go into that dark cupboard," said the shepherdess.

"I've heard that he has eleven china wives locked away in there already."

"Then you can be the twelfth," said the Mandarin. "For tonight, as soon as the cupboard starts creaking, you shall be married, as sure as I'm a Chinaman." And with that he nodded off to sleep.

The little shepherdess was in tears. She looked imploringly at her true love, the china chimney sweep, and said, "Please, take me out into the wide world. We can't stay here now."

"I'll do anything you want," the sweep replied. "Let's go at once. I feel sure I can earn enough to keep us, by working as a chimney sweep."

"If only we could get off the table," sighed the shepherdess. "I shall never be happy until we are out in the wide world."

He did his best to comfort her, and showed her where to place her foot on a piece of tracery to begin the climb down. He took his ladder, too, to help her in the difficult places; and at last they reached the floor. But when they looked up at the dark old cupboard – what an uproar! The carved deer were straining their necks out, waving their antlers and shaking their heads. And Brigadier-General Private Sergeant-Major Goatlegs was hopping up and down and shouting to the old Mandarin, "They're running away! They're running away!"

That gave them a fright, and they jumped out of harm's way into an open drawer. Inside they found three or four packs of cards – none of them quite complete – and a ramshackle toy theatre. The puppets were performing a play, and all the Queens – diamonds, hearts, clubs, and spades – were sitting in the front row fanning themselves with flowers. Behind them stood the Knaves, with their two heads, one at the top and one at the bottom; all playing cards are like that. They were watching a play about star-crossed lovers, and it made the shepherdess cry, because it was just like her own story.

"I can't bear it," she sobbed. "I must get out of this drawer" But by the time they got back to the floor again, the old Mandarin had woken up. He was rocking himself to and fro in a frenzy of nodding; that was the only way he could move.

"The old Mandarin is after us!" shrieked the little shepherdess. She was so frightened that she sank down onto her porcelain knees.

"I've got an idea," said the chimney sweep. "Let's creep into the big pot-pourri jar in the corner; we can hide on a bed of roses and lavender, and if he comes after us we can throw salt in his eyes."

"That wouldn't be any good," she said. "Besides, I happen to know that the old Mandarin and the pot-pourri jar were once engaged; and there is always some fellow-feeling left when people have been as close as that. There's nothing for it but to go out into the wide world."

"Are you really brave enough to come with me into the wide world?" asked the chimney sweep. "Do you realize how vast it is, and that we can never come back again?"

"Yes I do," she said.

The sweep looked her straight in the eyes. "The only path I know is up the chimney. Are you really brave enough to crawl right inside the stove, up the flue, and into the chimney? Once there, I can find the way. We must climb up and up, so high that no one can reach us; right at the top there's a hole that leads out into the wide world."

And he led her up to the door of the stove.

"How dark it looks!" she said. But she went with him all the same, past the firebricks and up the flue, into the pitch dark.

"Now we are in the chimney," he said. "Look up there! There's a lovely star twinkling above our heads."

Yes, there was a real star shining right down on them, as if to light their way. So they clambered and crawled toward it, up, up, up through the horrible dark. The sweep kept giving the shepherdess his hand, and showing her where to put her little china feet, until at last they reached the very top. They sat on the edge of the chimney pot, tired out, and no wonder.

Above them was the sky with all its stars; below was the town with all its roofs. The wide, wide world was all about them. The poor shepherdess had never dreamed it could be so vast; she laid her little head on the chimney sweep's shoulder, and wept so bitterly that her

tears washed the gold from her sash.

"It's all too much," she said "I can't bear it; the world is far too big. I wish I were back on the table below the mirror. I shall never be happy until we are back there again. I have followed you into the wide world; now if you love me, take me home."

The chimney sweep pleaded with her. He reminded her about the old Mandarin, and Brigadier-General Private Sergeant-Major Goatlegs, but that just made her cry even harder. She kissed him and clung to him, and finally he had to give in, though he knew it was a bad idea.

It was a hard and dangerous climb, down the chimney, through the flue, past the firebricks, and into the stove. There they paused, listening to hear what was happening. All was quiet, so they peeped out

Oh! There in the middle of the floor lay the old Chinese Mandarin. He had rocked himself right off the table, and was lying where he fell, smashed into three pieces – his back, his front, and his head, which had rolled off into a corner. Brigadier-General Private Sergeant-Major Goatlegs was just standing where he always did, deep in thought.

"How terrible," cried the little shepherdess. "Old Grandpa is broken to bits, and it's all our fault. I shall never forgive myself!" And she wrung her tiny hands.

"He can still be mended," said the chimney sweep. "That's not hard. Don't get in such a state. When they have glued him together, and put a rivet in his neck, he'll be as good as new, and able to give us a piece of his mind."

"Do you really think so?" she said. And then they climbed back up to the table top.

"We have been a long way," said the chimney sweep, "yet here we are back where we started. We might have saved ourselves the trouble."

"If only old Grandpa were mended," said the shepherdess. "Do you think it will be expensive?"

The family did have the Mandarin mended. His back was glued on; a rivet was put in his neck; he looked as good as new. But he couldn't nod his head any more.

"You have got high and mighty since you were broken," said Brigadier-General Private Sergeant-Major Goatlegs, "though I can't see what there is to be proud of in being glued. Tell me, am I to have her or not?"

The chimney sweep and the shepherdess looked anxiously at the old Mandarin; they were terrified that he might nod. But he had a rivet in his neck, and would never nod again, though he didn't want to admit that to a stranger. So the porcelain couple stayed together, and loved each other until they broke.

THE GOBLIN
AT THE GROCER'S

THERE was once a typical student who lived in the attic and didn't own a thing, and a typical grocer who lived downstairs and owned the whole house. There was a goblin, too, and the goblin moved in with the grocer, because every Christmas Eve the grocer gave him a big lump of butter. The grocer could easily afford it, and so the goblin stayed in the shop, as you can well understand.

One evening the student came in by the back door to buy a candle and a piece of cheese; he had to run his own errands. He made his purchases and exchanged a "good evening" nod with the grocer and his wife – a woman who could do more than just nod, for she had what they call the gift of the gab. As the student nodded, his eye fell on the piece of paper wrapped round the cheese. It was a page torn from an old book, a book that ought never to have been torn up – a book of poetry.

"There's more of that book if you want it," said the grocer. "I gave an old woman some coffee beans for it. I'll let you have it for a few pennies."

"Thanks," said the student. "I'll take the book instead of the cheese. Plain bread will do me fine, and it would be a shame for the rest of the book to be torn up. You are a good man, and a practical one, but you've as much sense of poetry as that barrel."

That was a rude thing to say – especially about the barrel – but both the grocer and the student laughed, because after all it was only said in fun. But the little goblin was annoyed that anyone should dare to speak like that to a grocer who owned the whole house and sold the best butter.

So that night, when the shop was shut and everyone but the student had gone to bed, the goblin sneaked into the bedroom and borrowed the grocer's wife's gift of the gab; she didn't need it while she was asleep. The goblin could lend the gift of the gab to anything and it would be able to speak its mind as well as you or me; but only one thing could have it at a time, which was just as well, or they'd all have spoken at once.

First the goblin lent the gift of the gab to the barrel where the grocer kept old newspapers for wrapping paper. "Is it really true," he asked, "that you have no sense of poetry?"

"Of course not," said the barrel. "I know all about it. It's the sort of thing they use to fill out the bottom of the page in a newspaper, and then people cut it out. I'm sure there's more poetry in me than in the student, and I'm only a humble barrel compared to the grocer."

Then the goblin lent the gift of the gab to the coffee mill – what a clatter! – the butter cask, and the till. They all agreed with the barrel, and the views of the majority have to be respected.

"Now for the student!" said the goblin, and he crept up the staircase to the attic where the student lived. The goblin peeked through the keyhole and saw the student reading the old book by the light of the candle.

How bright it was in there! A shaft of light was rising from the book, like a great shining tree which sheltered the student with its branches. Its leaves were a luminous green, and each flower was the

head of a lovely girl – some with dark flashing eyes, and some with clear blue ones. Each fruit was a shining star which rang and sang with beautiful music.

The little goblin had never dreamed of such music. So he stood there on tiptoe, enraptured, until the light in the attic went out. The student must have blown out the candle and gone to bed. But still the goblin lingered, listening as the fading echoes of the music lulled the student to sleep.

"That was amazing!" said the goblin. "I never expected that! I think I'll stay with the student." He thought it over long and hard, and then he sighed, "But the student hasn't got any butter!" So he went – yes, he went back down to the shop, and it was just as well he did, for the barrel had nearly worn out the gift of the gab, telling all the news that was inside it from one angle, and then turning round and telling it all over again from another.

The goblin took the gift of the gab back to the grocer's wife. But from then on, the whole shop, from the till to the firewood, deferred to the barrel. They held it in such high regard that in future, when the grocer read out articles from the newspaper, they thought he must have learned it all from the barrel.

But the little goblin wasn't satisfied anymore to sit and listen to the talk downstairs, however wise and well informed it was. As soon as the light glimmered down from the attic, it seemed to draw him to it by invisible cables. He just had to go and look through the keyhole.

Whenever he did, a sense of unutterable grandeur surged through him – the kind of feeling you get when God rides his storm clouds across the thundering sea. The goblin would burst into tears. He couldn't have said what he was crying for, but it comforted him. How wonderful it would be to sit with the student under that tree! But it was not to be – he had to make do with the keyhole.

He stood there on the chilly landing, but he never noticed the cold until the light went out and the music had faded away into the wind. Then he shivered! He was glad to get back to his warm corner downstairs, where he was so snug. And there was the Christmas butter to look forward to. Yes – the grocer was the one!

But in the middle of the night the goblin was woken by a terrible commotion. People in the street were banging on the shutters, and the watchman was blowing his whistle. "Fire! Fire!"

The whole street was lit up by flames. But where was the fire? Here, or next door? Everyone panicked. The grocer's wife was so flustered that she took off her gold earrings and put them in her pocket, to be sure of saving something. The grocer hunted frantically for his share certificates, and the maid ran to fetch the silk scarf she had saved up to buy. Everyone wanted to save the thing they cared about most.

The goblin was no different. He sprang up the stairs into the attic room, where the student was standing quietly looking out of the window at the fire across the road. The goblin grabbed the precious book from the table, wrapped it in his red cap, and held onto it with both hands. The house's greatest treasure was safe!

Off he ran, up to the roof and onto the highest chimney pot. And there he sat, cradling the book in his hands, while the fire over the way lit up the sky. He knew now where his heart lay, and where he really belonged.

When the fire was put out, the goblin had time to reflect.

Yes! "I'll divide my time between them," he said. "I can't forsake the grocer – because of the butter."

And that was very human! Because we, too, have to go to the grocer – for the butter.

THE SHADOW

IN the hot countries, the sun really knows how to shine – it scorches down so hard it turns the people quite brown.

This story is about a clever young man – a philosopher – who came from the cold north to the hot south. At first he thought he could wander about just as if he were at home, but he soon learned better. During the day, he, like all sensible people, stayed in his apartment with the shutters closed. It was as if they were all asleep, or there was no one at home.

The worst of it was that the narrow street of tall houses in which he lived was open all day to the full glare of the sun. It was awful; the young philosopher felt as if he were sweltering in an oven. He really couldn't bear it. He began to waste away, and so did his shadow, for the blazing sun affected that too; it was much smaller here than at home. It was only after the sun went down that the man and his shadow began to revive.

That was a sight to see! As soon as the lamp was brought into the room, the shadow stretched itself right up the wall until it touched the ceiling; it had to stretch to get its strength back. The young stranger used to go out onto the balcony to have his stretch. As he watched the stars twinkling through the cool clear air, he felt the life tingling back into his veins.

All along the street, people were coming out onto their balconies to taste the air. Up on the balconies, and down on the street, the city came to life. Tailors and shoemakers moved out onto the street; chairs and tables were fetched outside, and lamps lit; some shouted, some sang; everywhere people were strolling, or driving in carriages; a tinkling *ting-a-ling-a-ling* sounded from the bells on donkeys' harnesses. Little boys were letting off fireworks; church bells were ringing; a funeral passed through the street – yes, it was all going on down there!

Only one house remained silent – the house directly opposite the young philosopher's. Yet someone must live there, because beautiful flowers grew on the balcony, and they would wither up in the hot sun if they weren't watered. Besides, in the evening the balcony door was left open, and although it seemed quite dark inside – certainly in the front room – the young man could hear music from within. He thought the music utterly beautiful – but then, he thought everything was wonderful in that hot country, except for the sun. He asked his landlord who lived there, but he didn't know; as for the music, the landlord thought it was an annoying racket: "Just like someone playing the same piece over and over again, telling themselves, 'This time I will get it right!' But they won't, however hard they try."

One night the stranger woke up. He was sleeping with the balcony door open, and the curtain had been blown aside by the breeze. A light was shining from the balcony opposite, lighting up the flowers. In the heart of the glow stood a slim, graceful girl, with a glory about her that dazzled the eyes. In a moment he was wide awake He leaped from his bed and up to the curtain – but the girl was gone, the light was gone.

Through the open door, music was drifting, music so soft and enchanting that it left him rapt in thought. It was a kind of magic.

Who could be living there? The young man couldn't even see where the entrance to the apartment was, for the whole ground floor was taken up with shops.

One evening, the stranger was sitting on his balcony with a lamp burning behind him. So naturally, his shadow fell upon the wall opposite; right among the flowers on the balcony. And when the stranger moved, the shadow moved, as shadows will.

"I believe my shadow is the only living thing over there," said the young man. "It looks really at home among the flowers, And the door is ajar – what a chance for the shadow to nip in and have a look-see; then it could come and tell me all about it." He looked right at the shadow. "Now then, look lively," he said, only joking. "Step inside! Well, aren't you going?" And he gave the shadow a nod, and the shadow nodded back. "Off you go," said the stranger, "but mind you come back." The stranger stood up, and the shadow stood up. The stranger turned round, and the shadow turned round. And anyone watching would have seen the shadow slip through the half-open balcony door, just as the stranger went back into his room, and closed the curtains behind him.

Next morning the philosopher went out to get a coffee and read the papers. "What's this?" he exclaimed, as he walked into the sunshine. "Where's my shadow? Don't say it really did go off exploring last night, and hasn't returned. What a bore."

That evening, he went out once again onto his balcony, with the light behind him, knowing that a shadow always likes its master to act as a screen. But he couldn't fetch it back. He stretched, and crouched, but no shadow fell. He stood and coughed meaningfully – "*Ahem! Ahem!*" – but it did no good.

It was all very irritating. But in the hot countries everything grows very fast. Only a week later, the stranger noticed, when he stepped into the sun, that he was growing a new shadow, from the roots of the old one. He was delighted. In three weeks, he had quite a respectable shadow again. As he made his way home to the north, the new shadow grew yet more, until it was bigger than he really needed.

So the young philosopher settled down in his cold homeland, and wrote books about everything that is true, and good, and beautiful in the world. The days, weeks, and years passed – many years.

One evening, when he was sitting in his study, he heard a discreet knock at the door. He called out, "Come in," but no-one entered. So he got up and opened the door. The man who stood there gave him an uncomfortable feeling. He was so very thin. But he was dressed smartly, and was obviously a man of rank.

"Who are you?" asked the philosopher.

"I thought you wouldn't recognize me," said the skinny visitor. "I've filled out so much – in fact, I've become a man of substance. I dare say you never thought I'd do so well for myself. Don't you know your own old shadow? I can see you thought I'd gone for good. But here I am. I'll have you know I'm quite rich – I can buy my freedom, if it's necessary." So saying he fingered the heavy gold chain he was wearing round his neck, and showed off the diamond rings that sparkled on his fingers. They were all real!

"You've taken my breath away!" said the philosopher. "What does all this mean?"

"It is out of the ordinary," replied the shadow, "but then, you are by

no means an ordinary man, and from our earliest memories I walked in your footsteps. When you thought I was able to make my own way in the world, I set out alone. I've done very well for myself, but nevertheless I've lately found myself longing to see you once more before you die – for you must die one day. Also, I wanted to revisit the land of my childhood. By the way, I see you've found yourself a new shadow. Do I owe you or it anything? Please let me know."

"Is it really you?" said the philosopher "What a turn-up for the books! Who would have thought my old shadow would come knocking on my door?"

"Tell me what I owe you," repeated the shadow. "I don't like to be in anyone's debt."

"Stop babbling about debts," said the philosopher. "You owe me nothing. You are as free as air; I'm just delighted to hear of your good fortune. Sit down, old friend, and tell me all about it – and first, tell me what happened that night in the house across the street."

"Very well," said the shadow, sitting down "But first promise me that you will not tell anyone in this town that I was once your shadow. I am thinking of getting married – I could support a family."

"Of course I won't tell," said the philosopher. "My lips are sealed; I give you my word – and a man's only as good as his word."

"So is a shadow," came the reply.

It was amazing, really, how human the shadow had become. He was dressed all in black, but everything was of the finest quality, from his shining leather boots to his smart black hat. What with his gold chain and his diamond rings, the shadow was very well turned out; it was the clothes that made the man.

"Now I shall begin," said the shadow, stamping his boots firmly down on the philosopher's new shadow, which was lying like a poodle at his feet. It may just have been pride; or maybe he was hoping the shadow would attach itself to him. The new shadow just lay there, quite still, hanging on every word: it wanted to learn how it might free itself, and be its own master.

"Who do you think it was living in that house?" asked the shadow.

"It was the fairest of all – it was Poetry! I was there for three weeks, and that's as good as living for three thousand years, and reading everything that was imagined or written in all that time. Believe me, it's true I've seen all, and I know all!"

"Poetry!" cried the philosopher. "Yes, often she lives a quiet life in the heart of the bustling city. I glimpsed her once, when I was still half-asleep. She dazzled my eyes, as she stood on the balcony, radiant as the northern lights. Go on, please. You were on the balcony, you slipped through the door, and then . . ."

"I found myself in an entrance hall; that's what you were looking at all that time. There was no lamp; it was dark. But there was a long row of rooms leading off it, all lit by the glare from the innermost room, where Poetry lived. That was so bright it would have snuffed out a shadow, so I took my time approaching it – as everyone should."

"Yes, yes, but get on with the story!" snapped the philosopher.

"I saw everything, and I will tell you about it," replied the shadow, "but first I must ask you to show some respect. I'm not a snob, but I am a free man, and a man of learning, not to speak of my position in society, and I'll thank you to remember it."

"You're right, sir," said the philosopher "I was at fault, and I will bear what you say in mind. Now, please tell me everything you saw."

"Everything?" said the shadow. "I saw all, and I know all."

"What did Poetry's inner room look like?" asked the philosopher.

"Like a grove of forest trees? Or a vaulted church? Or like the starlit heavens seen from a mountain top?"

"I didn't go right inside," replied the shadow "I stayed in the twilit hall, and peered in from there. It was a good vantage point. I saw everything; I know everything. I have been in Poetry's entrance hall."

"Yes, but what did you see? Did you see the ancient gods and heroes striding through those great halls? Did you see the children playing, and telling each other their dreams?"

"I was there, I tell you, and I saw everything. What you would have made of it, I do not know, but it turned me into a man. I learned about my own nature, and its inborn poetry. When I lived with you, I never thought of these things. When the sun rose and set, you will remember, I grew uncommonly tall – by moonlight, I was almost more plain to see than you. But I didn't understand, until I was standing there in Poetry's entrance hall, and then I realized – I was a man. I left the place transformed.

"By then, you had left for home. I was ashamed, as a man, to be seen about in my condition. I needed boots and clothes – all the outer trappings by which a man is judged. I hid – I can trust you not to put this in a book – under the skirts of a woman who sold cakes in the market; I didn't come out until nightfall. Then I ran along the street in the moonlight, and stretched myself up against the wall – it did my back good. I ran up and down, peeping into rooms, high and low. I peeped where no one else could peep; I saw what no one else could see – what no one ever should see.

"What a sorry world this is. I wouldn't want to be a man, if people didn't value it so. I saw ugly, unbelievable things done by husbands and wives, mothers and fathers, even by little children. I saw what no one should ever see, but everyone wants to see – people's dirty secrets. If I had published them in a newspaper, I should have had plenty of readers! But instead I wrote privately to each individual; that made them quake in their boots. Everywhere I went, I threw them into a panic. They feared me, so they fawned on me. The professors made me a professor, the tailors gave me new clothes – you see how well I dress

– the coiners minted coins for me, all the women admired me. And that's what made me the man I am today.

"I must be going. Here's my card. I live on the sunny side of the street, and am always at home when it rains." And the shadow left.

"Strange," said the philosopher. "How strange!"

Days, years passed – the shadow came again.

"How are things?" he asked

"I still write about the good, the true, and the beautiful," replied the philosopher, "but no one seems to care. It makes me sick at heart, for these things mean the world to me."

"I never think of them," said the shadow. "I've been concentrating on getting fat; that's what matters. You just don't understand the world, that's what's wrong with you. You should travel. I'm planning a trip abroad this summer; why not come with me? I would like a companion – you could come as my shadow! It really would be fun, and I would pay for everything."

"That's a bit much," said the philosopher.

"Not at all," replied the shadow "It would do you the world of good to travel. If you went as my shadow, it wouldn't cost you a thing."

"It's absurd!"

"Maybe it is, but so is the world, and it always has been." And with that the shadow went away.

Things didn't go well with the philosopher. He was dogged by worry and grief. Whenever he talked about the true, the good, and the beautiful, people looked at him like a cow that's just been offered a bunch of roses. In the end his health failed.

"You're a shadow of your former self," his friends told him, and it sent a chill right through him.

"You should go and take a cure at a health spa," said the shadow, when he dropped in one day. "That's the thing for you. I'll take you with me for old time's sake, and bear all the expenses. You can write an account of our travels, and keep me amused on the journey. I want to go to a spa anyway, as my beard won't grow. That's just as much an illness as anything else – a man needs a beard. Do come with me."

So they set off together, only this time the shadow was the master and the master was the shadow. Whether they were driving in a coach, riding, or walking, the shadow always put himself in the master's place in the line of the sun; though the good-natured philosopher never noticed.

One day the philosopher said, "I've been turning over in my mind what you said when we first met again, that I didn't show you enough respect. Since then, we've been formal with each other. But now that we are companions, and have known each other since childhood, I would like us to clasp hands, and call each other friend, and be easy in our speech once more."

"That's all very well," said the shadow. "You've been frank; I shall be so too. As a philosopher, you must know how fussy people can be. Some can't abide brown paper; others are set on edge when someone runs a fingernail down a pane of glass. That's how I feel when you talk to me in a familiar manner. It rubs me up the wrong way. It's as if you're reminding me of our former relations. I'm not a snob; it's just the way I feel. So I can't let you speak to me without showing respect; but I'm quite willing to meet you halfway, and talk to you without any respect at all."

"This is a pretty pass," thought the philosopher, "that I must 'Sir' him while he calls me names." But he had to put up with it.

At last they came to the spa. There were plenty of people there taking the waters, among them a princess, whose problem was that she saw too clearly for comfort.

The princess noticed at once that the newcomer was different from all the others. "They say he's here because his beard won't grow," she said to herself, "but really it must be because he can't cast a shadow."

She was dying to know the truth, so when she saw him out walking, she went straight up to him, in the direct way princesses have, and said, "Your trouble is that you have no shadow."

"Your Royal Highness must be getting better," he replied. "I know that you are too clear-sighted, but you must be cured. I do indeed have a shadow, though an unusual one: that's him over there. Ordinary people have ordinary shadows, but I am not an ordinary person. Just as grand folk dress their servants in the finest livery, so I have decked my shadow out as a human being. If you look, you'll see I've even given him a shadow of his own. It was expensive, but worth it for he's one of a kind."

"Have I really been cured?" wondered the princess. "If so, the waters here must be miraculous. But even so, there's no need to hurry away, just as things are getting interesting here. I do hope this man's beard doesn't grow too quickly."

In the ballroom that evening, the princess danced with the shadow. She was as light as a feather, but he was lighter still; she had never had such a partner. She told him where she came from, and it turned out he had once visited the country, when she had been abroad. He had peeped in at all sorts of windows, and seen all sorts of things. He told her some of these, and hinted at others, and quite amazed her. She thought he must know more than anyone else in the world.

By the second dance, she was in love. The shadow knew it, for she began to look right through him. During the third dance, she nearly told him, but she kept her head, remembering her duty to her country and her people. "He knows the ways of the world," she thought, "and that's good. He's a beautiful dancer, and that's better still. But is he wise? That's the most important thing of all." So she began to ask him hard questions, which she couldn't have answered herself.

The shadow's face clouded over. "You can't answer!" she said.

"I could," said the shadow, "but these are children's riddles. I believe even my old shadow could answer them."

"Your shadow," said the princess. "That would be remarkable."

"I don't promise," said the shadow, "but I think he could. After all, he's been following me around all these years, and hearing everything I say. Yes – I think he could do it. But, a word to the wise, Your Highness, he is so proud of people taking him for a man; if you treat him as one, you'll get the best out of him."

"It will be my pleasure," said the princess.

So she joined the philosopher by the door, and quizzed him about the sun and the moon and human beings, inside and out, and his answers were both learned and wise.

"What a man this must be, when his shadow knows so much," she thought. "And what a blessing to my people and my country if I married him! I shall do it."

The princess and the shadow soon came to an understanding, but they decided to keep it a secret until the princess got home. "I won't even tell my shadow," said the shadow, no doubt he had his own reasons for that.

At last they came to the princess's country.

"Now listen to me, friend," said the shadow to the philosopher. "I am now as rich and as powerful as a man can be, and I want you to share in my good fortune. You shall live with me in the palace, and ride with me in the royal coach, and be well paid for it. But you must let everybody call you 'Shadow,' and never tell anyone that you were once a man; and once a year, when I sit in the sun on the balcony to show myself to the people, you must lie at my feet like a good shadow. You know, I am marrying the princess this very evening."

"It's wrong!" said the philosopher. "I won't do it. You'd be cheating the people, never mind the princess. I'm going to tell the truth: that I am a man, and you are a mere shadow, just dressed like one."

"It won't do any good," said the shadow. "No one will believe you. Do be sensible, or I'll have to call the guard."

"I'm going straight to the princess."

"But I'm going first," said the shadow, "and you're going to prison. Guard!"

And to prison he went, for of course the guard obeyed the princess's betrothed.

"You're trembling," said the princess, when the shadow found her. "Has something happened? You're not coming down with something, on our wedding day?"

"I've had a terrible shock," said the shadow. "It's my poor shadow – I can hardly believe it – I suppose it's all been too much for his shadow-brain – he's gone quite mad! He's convinced himself that he really is a man, and – if you can believe it – that I am his shadow."

"How awful," said the princess. "I hope he's safely locked up."

"For his own good I fear he may never recover."

"Poor shadow!" said the princess. "How sad. Perhaps it would be a kindness to put him out of his misery. Now I think of it, I'm sure that would be the best course – just to put him to sleep without any fuss."

"It seems hard," said the shadow, "for he was a faithful servant."

And he pursed his lips and made a sound like a sigh.

"You are noble," said the princess.

That night the whole city was lit up. Cannons were fired – *Boom! Boom! Boom!* Soldiers presented arms. What a wedding it was! At the end the shadow and the princess came out onto the balcony, and the people cheered them to the skies.

The philosopher didn't hear it; he had already been put to death.

IN A THOUSAND YEARS' TIME

Written in 1853

Y ES, in a thousand years' time, people will fly across the ocean on wings of steam. The young citizens of America will come to pay their respects to old Europe. They will come to see our monuments and our decaying cities, just as nowadays we tour the crumbling glories of South Asia.

In a thousand years' time, they will come.

The Thames, the Danube, and the Rhine will still be rolling on; Mont Blanc will still be wearing its cap of snow; the northern lights will still play across the northlands. Generation after generation will have come to dust. The great men of our day will be as forgotten as the Viking chieftain whose funeral mound some prosperous farmer has turned into a viewpoint where he can sit and gaze out over his waving fields of corn.

"To Europe!" cry the young Americans. "To the land of our fathers, to the wonderland land of memories and dreams – to Europe!"

Here comes the airship. It will be crowded, for it is much faster to fly than to sail. The electro-magnetic cable under the ocean has already telegraphed ahead the passenger list on the air caravan.

The coast of Ireland is reached first; but the passengers are still asleep; they are not woken until they arrive in England. There they will set foot in the land of Shakespeare, as the cultured ones call it; the others call it the land of Democracy, or the land of the Industrial Revolution.

The tourists will devote a whole day to England and Scotland; then their journey continues through the Channel Tunnel to France, the country of Charlemagne and Napoleon. Some of them have heard of Molière, too, but the arguments of the classical and romantic schools are all in the past; the names on the tourists' lips are of celebrities, poets, and scientists of whom our age has never heard – they have yet to be born, in that cradle of Europe, Paris.

The airship will then fly over the country from which Columbus sailed, where Cortés was born, and where Calderón composed his dramas in flowing verse. Beautiful dark-eyed women still live in its fertile valleys, and their folk songs still name El Cid and the palace of Alhambra.

Through the air once more, to Italy, where the Eternal City of Rome once stood. It has been wiped out. The Campagna is a desert; one wall of St. Peter's is still standing, but there are doubts whether it is genuine.

Then to Greece, to spend a night in the luxury hotel on Mount Olympus – just to say that they have been there. Next stop is the Bosporus, for a few hours' rest on the site of Byzantium. A handful of poor fishermen spreading their nets still remember old tales of the harems that stood here in days gone by.

Then the airship flies along the Danube, allowing glimpses of ruined cities below, cities our age never knew. Every now and then the ship will land to allow the tourists to admire some monument that belongs to their past, but our future.

Then the airship is aloft again. Below lies Germany, which was once crisscrossed by railroads and canals – Germany, the land where Luther spoke, and Goethe sang, and Mozart made his music. But when they speak of science and arts, their talk will be of names we do not know.

One day is given to Germany, and one to the whole of Scandinavia –
the homelands of Ørsted and Linnaeus, and Norway, the young country
of the old heroes. Iceland is a stop on the homeward journey. The
geyser no longer spouts, and the volcano has died, but the rocky island
still stands in the foaming sea, the memorial stone of the sagas.

"There's a lot to see in Europe," say the young Americans. "You
need a whole week, a So-and-so has shown in his guidebook, *See
Europe in Seven Days*."

IT'S PERFECTLY TRUE

"WHAT'S the world coming to?" asked a hen – who lived on the other side of town from where it all happened. "The goings-on in the henhouse – it's quite shocking. It's just as well that there are so many of us roosting together; I wouldn't get a wink of sleep on my own." And then she told them the story. It made the other hen's feathers stand on end, and the rooster's comb flop over. It's perfectly true!

But let's begin at the beginning. It was in the henhouse on the other side of town. The sun was setting, and the hens were settling on their roost. One of them was a stumpy-legged bird with white feathers; she laid an egg every day, and was altogether a model of respectability. When she flew up to the roost, she plumed herself with her beak, and a little feather fell out.

"Let it go!" she said. "The more I preen the lovelier I will grow." All this was said in fun, for – despite being so respectable – she was a hen with a merry heart. And then she went to sleep.

It was dark; hen nestled up to hen; but the one next to the one who had lost a feather was not asleep. She had both heard and not heard what was said – as you must often do if you want a quiet life. But she

couldn't keep what she had heard to herself. She said to the next hen along, "Did you hear that? Naming no names, a certain hen in this roost means to pluck out all her feathers; it's the fashion. If I were a rooster, I wouldn't look twice at her."

Right above the henhouse lived a family of owls. With their sharp ears they could hear every word that the hen said. The mother rolled her eyes, and fanned herself with her wings. "Don't listen! But I suppose you must have heard what she said? I could hardly believe my ears! One of the hens has so forgotten all decency that she is calmly plucking off all her feathers, in full view of the rooster!"

"*Prenez garde aux enfants!*" said the father owl. "Not in front of the children!"

"But I must tell my friend across the way," said the mother. "She has to hear this." And away she flew.

"*Tu-whit, tu-whoo! Tu-whit, tu-whoo!*" The mother owl and her friend hooted over the tale; and it carried right down to the dovecot. "Have you heard the latest? *Tu-whit, tu-whoo!* A hen has plucked out all her feathers to please the rooster. She'll freeze to death, if she hasn't died already."

"Where, where?" cooed the doves.

"In the yard over there. I as good as saw it with my own eyes. The story's scarcely fit to be told, but it's perfectly true!"

"True, true!" cooed the doves "Perfectly true!" And they took the story down to the henhouse in their yard. "There's a hen – some say there were two of them – and they've plucked out all their feathers so that they'll stand out from the crowd and attract the rooster. But they're playing with fire, for it's easy to catch a chill, and a chill can turn to a fever; in fact, they're both dead, the pair of them."

That gave the rooster a jolt. "Wake up! Wake up!" he crowed, and he flew up onto the fence post. His eyes were still full of sleep, but he crowed anyway: "Three hens have died for love of a rooster! They plucked out all their feathers! It's a scandal – I won't hush it up – pass it on!"

"Pass it on! Pass it on!" piped the bats. "Pass it on!" clucked the hens. "Pass it on!" crowed the roosters. And so the story went from henhouse to henhouse, right round town, until it came back to the very spot where it started.

"There are five hens," the tale now ran, "who have plucked off all their feathers, to show which of them had wasted away the most for love of a rooster. Then they pecked each other to death. It's a great shame for their family, and a serious loss for their owner."

The hen that had lost just one little feather didn't recognize her own story. As she was a respectable hen, she said, "I despise those hens! And there are others like them. Such things shouldn't be kept secret. I'm going to write to the papers about it, and then the whole country will hear about it – and serve those hens right, and their family too."

The story was published in the newspaper, and – as it was in print – it must be perfectly true!

"*One little feather can become five hens!*"

DANCE, DANCE, DOLLY MINE!

"THAT must be a song for very little children," declared Aunt Malle. "I think it's silly, that 'Dance, dance, dolly mine!'"

But little Amalie liked it – she was only three years old, and she was always playing with her dolls. She was bringing them up to be as clever as Aunt Malle.

There was a student who came to the house to help Amalie's brothers with their homework, and he often took the time to talk to Amalie and her dolls. He wasn't like anyone else – Amalie thought he was very funny. Aunt Malle said he had no idea how to speak to children – their little heads couldn't possibly take in his tomfoolery. But little Amalie's could – she even learned by heart all the words of his ditty, 'Dance, dance, dolly mine!' and sang it to her three dolls. Two of them were new – a girl and a boy – but the third was old. Her name was Lisa, and she liked listening to the song because she was mentioned in it.

Dance, dance, dolly mine!
Oh, you look so very fine!
And your boyfriend looks good too,
In trousers of white and jacket of blue –
He wears his hat and gloves just so,
And shoes so tight they pinch his toe.
He is fine and she is fine,
Dance, dance, dolly mine!

Look, look, Lisa's here,
My dear dolly from last year!
She has brand-new flaxen hair
And a face that's clean and fair.
She really looks quite young again –
Come to me, my old friend.
You must join the fun, and so
The three of you – put on a show.

Dance, dance, my dollies bright,
Get the steps and rhythms right.
Keep your back straight, don't forget,
Point your toe and pirouette.
The dance is nearly over now –
Leap, twirl, and take a bow.
You really are a sight to see –
Dance, dance, my dollies three.

The dolls understood the song, little Amalie understood it, and the student understood it, too – but then, he had written it, and he said it was an excellent song. Only Aunt Malle did not understand it – she had long since climbed the fence between childhood and adulthood, so she thought it was nonsense. But little Amalie didn't agree, and she kept on singing the song.

It is from her singing that we have it.

GRIEF

This story is in two parts. The first part's not really necessary, but it makes a good foundation, and that's always a help.

We were staying at a manor house in the country, and our host was away for the day. Along came a widow woman from the nearby town, with a pug dog under her arm. She said she'd come to sell shares in her tannery. She had all her papers with her. We told her to put them in an envelope and address it to the owner of the house, with all his titles: Commissary General, Sir, and so on.

She put pen to paper, and then paused. She asked us to repeat the address, a bit more slowly. She started to write it out, but bang in the middle of the word "Commissary" she got stuck. "I'm only a woman!" she said.

The pug, which she had put down on the floor, started to growl. He had accompanied her for the outing, and for the sake of his health, but he hadn't bargained on being put on the floor. He was a podgy, snub-nosed pug.

"He won't bite," said the woman. "He's got no teeth. He's like one of the family. He's faithful, and if he's cranky, it's my grandchildren's fault. They tease him, making him be the bridesmaid when they play at

weddings; he finds it all a strain, the poor old boy."

Then she handed in her papers, picked up the pug, and left.

That's the first part of the story, the part we could have left out.

The pug dog died – that's the second part.

It was about a week later. We were visiting the town, and staying at an inn. Our rooms looked over the back yard, which was divided in two by a wooden fence. On one side, hides were hanging to dry; it was the widow's tannery.

The pug dog had died that very morning, and been buried in the yard. The grandchildren – that's the widow's grandchildren, not the pug's, for the pug had never married – were putting the final touches to the grave; it was a fine grave – a pleasure to lie in.

It had an edging of broken pots, and it was covered with sand. For a tombstone there was a broken beer-bottle, neck upwards, though that didn't mean anything.

The children danced around the grave, and the eldest boy, a likely lad of seven, suggested that they should exhibit the grave to anyone in the street who would like to see it: admission, one trouser button. Every boy could afford that, and pay for a girl too. Everyone agreed.

All the children from the street, and the back alley too, came, and paid their buttons. Quite a few trousers were in danger of falling down that afternoon, but it was worth it, to see the pug dog's grave.

Outside the yard, pressed up against the gate, stood a little, ragged girl. She was lovely, with curly hair and clear blue eyes. She didn't say a word, or shed a tear, but every time the gate opened she peeked in. She didn't have a button, so she had to stand there while all the other children had their look at the grave. When the last one left, she sat down on the ground, put her head in her hands, and sobbed her heart out; she was the only one who hadn't seen the pug dog's grave. That was grief, as heart-rending for her as any grown-up sorrow.

We watched from above. And from above, her trouble, like our own, might seem a joke.

That's the story. Anyone who doesn't understand it had better take shares in the widow's tannery.

THE
GARDENER AND
HIS MASTER

A FEW miles from the capital stood an old manor house with thick walls, towers, and stepped gables. It was the summer home of a rich nobleman and his wife; it was the best and handsomest of all the houses they owned. It was so well kept it looked as if it was new built, and inside it was comfortable and welcoming. The family arms were carved in stone over the entrance, surrounded by climbing roses.

The garden in front of the house was laid to lawn, with both pink and white may trees. There were even rare flowers of the kind you usually see in a greenhouse, for the nobleman employed a skilled gardener. The flower garden, the orchard, even the kitchen garden were delightful. By the kitchen garden you could still make out some of the original garden design, with box hedges clipped into the shape of crowns and pyramids. Beyond that towered two ancient trees, almost bare leaves, that looked as if the wind had been pelting them with great lumps of muck – but every lump was a bird's nest.

Here, for time out of mind, rooks and crows had built their nests. The two old trees were a regular settlement of screaming birds. They were the oldest family on the estate, and they regarded themselves as its true masters. They scorned the flightless creatures below, and didn't pay them much attention except when they started banging away with their guns, when the birds would flap into the air squawking *Caw! Caw!*

The gardener often suggested cutting the trees down, as they were an eyesore, and if they were gone, the screaming birds would go, too. But the master wouldn't hear of it, for the trees and the birds were part of the garden – something from the old days, that shouldn't just be thrown away.

"Those trees belong to the birds now. Leave them alone, my good Larsen," he would say. The gardener's name was Larsen, though that's neither here nor there. "Haven't you got enough to do already, Larsen, what with the flower garden, the orchard, the kitchen garden, and the greenhouse?"

It was true, the gardener was responsible for all these, and he worked hard and well. The master and mistress knew this, but all the same they couldn't resist telling him every now and then how they had seen flowers or eaten fruit at other people's houses that were better than anything in their garden. The gardener was always cast down at this, for he did his best. He had a good heart, and he was good at his job.

One day the master sent for him and told him – in a friendly but patronizing way – that the day before, while dining with some distinguished friends, they had been served apples and pears so juicy and mouthwatering that all the guests had been really impressed. The fruit was obviously not homegrown, but if it would stand the climate, it should be imported. As the fruit was known to have been bought at the city's leading greengrocer's, the gardener should ride in and find out

where the apples and pears were from, and order cuttings.

The gardener knew the greengrocer's well, for that was where, with his master's permission, he sold off the surplus fruit and vegetables from the garden. So he went to town and asked the greengrocer where he had got the apples and pears that he had so admired.

"Why, they were from your own garden!" said the greengrocer. He showed the gardener some of the fruit, and he recognized it at once.

The gardener was thrilled. He hurried home and told his master the good news that the fruit came from his own garden.

But the master and mistress wouldn't believe it. "There must be some mistake, Larsen. Go and get the greengrocer to put it in writing."

So Larsen got a written certificate from the greengrocer.

"How strange!" said the master.

From then on, the dining table at the manor always had a great bowl filled with apples and pears from the garden. The master had fruit crated up and sent as presents to friends in the city and elsewhere – some even overseas. What an excitement! Though they had to admit that it had been an unusually good year for fruit trees across the country.

Some time later the master and mistress were invited to dine with the king. The next day, they sent for the gardener. The king had served some exquisite melons from the royal greenhouse.

"You must go to the royal gardener, Larsen, and ask him for some melon seeds."

"But the royal gardener got his seeds from us," said Larsen, highly delighted.

"Then the man has improved the fruit in some way," snapped the master. "Every melon was perfect."

"I'm very pleased to hear it," said Larsen. "I should explain that the royal gardener has had no luck with his melons this year. When he saw ours, he begged three of them for the king's table."

"Do you mean to say that we were eating our own melons?"

"I'm sure you were." And Larsen went to the royal gardener and got him to write a certificate confirming that the king's melons had come from the manor garden.

The master was quite taken aback. But soon he was showing the certificate around, and sending melon seeds far and wide, just as he had with the apples and pears.

The seeds were a great success, and they were named after the manor house – so now the house's name was known in England, Germany, and France. Who would have thought it?

"I do hope the gardener won't let it go to his head," said the master.

He didn't; but he did want to become one of the best gardeners in the land. Each year he tried to excel at something, and he often succeeded. But people often said that nothing was ever quite as good as his very first fruit, the apples and pears. The melons, of course, were good in their way; his strawberries were all very well, but no bigger or juicier than those to be found elsewhere.

The year the radishes failed, no one could talk of anything else, although other things had turned out well. It was almost as if the master felt quite relieved to be able to say, "A poor year, Larsen." It pleased him to say it: "A poor year."

Twice a week the gardener would take fresh flowers up to the house. He arranged them with great skill, so that nothing clashed; each bouquet was a delight.

"You're blessed with good taste, Larsen," said the mistress. "Though of course that's a gift from God, and nothing to be proud of."

One day his arrangement was a crystal bowl with a water lily leaf floating on the surface. On top of this, with its stalk going down into the water, was a brilliant blue flower as big as a sunflower.

"An Indian lotus flower!" exclaimed the mistress. She had never seen anything like it.

The bowl was placed where the sun would catch it in the daytime, and it would reflect the candlelight at night. Everyone who saw it thought it was as lovely as it was unusual.

The young princess – who was good and kind – admired it so much that the master and mistress gave it to her to take back to the royal castle. Then they went into the garden to try to pick another for themselves; but they couldn't find one. So they called the gardener and asked him where he had got the Indian lotus flower from. "We've looked everywhere," they said. "It's not in the greenhouse or in the flower garden."

"No, it's not," said the gardener. "It is only a humble flower from the kitchen garden. But all the same, it's lovely isn't it? It's like a blue cactus, the flower of the artichoke."

"You should have made that perfectly clear," said the master, "instead of letting us think it was a rare foreign flower. Now you've shown us up in front of the princess. She was so taken with the flower that we gave it to her. She knows a lot about botany, and she didn't know what it was; but then, botany doesn't have anything to do with vegetables. My good Larsen, how could you have sent such a thing into the house? You've made fools of us."

So the beautiful blue flower from the kitchen garden was banished from the manor house, where it didn't belong. The master sent his

apologies to the princess, explaining that the lotus flower was nothing but a common vegetable. It was the gardener's fault, and he had been given a good dressing down for his impudence.

"What a shame! It's not fair," said the princess. "He has opened our eyes to a beautiful flower that we had overlooked. I will order the royal gardener to bring me an artichoke flower every day, for as long as they are in bloom."

And she did; so the master and mistress told Larsen that, after all, he might bring them another artichoke blossom. "It really is a remarkable flower," they said, and they complimented Larsen on it.

"Larsen loves praise," they said. "He's like a spoiled child."

That autumn there was a violent storm. A number of trees on the estate were torn up by the roots. To the master's regret, the two ancient trees with the birds' nests were among those that were blown down. The birds beat on the manor windows with their wings, shrieking with anger.

"I suppose you're happy now, Larsen," said the master. "The storm has brought the trees down, and the birds have fled to the wood. Soon there'll be nothing left to remind us of the old days. It's very sad."

The gardener said nothing. He had long ago thought what he would do with this sunny area once the trees were gone. He meant to make it the most beautiful part of the garden.

The big trees had destroyed the old topiary hedges in their fall. In their place, he planted shrubs and trees from the countryside – the kind of plants no other gardener would think worthy of a garden. Each was planted in shade or sunshine, depending where it would thrive, and all were tended with loving care.

Junipers from the heaths of Jutland raised themselves high like

Italian cypresses. The wild green holly was a delight to the eye in summer and winter. Ferns of many kinds grew like miniature palm trees. The burdock – which is despised as a weed – blossomed with flowers worthy of any bouquet. In damper soil, the common dock spread out its sculptural leaves. Mulleins like giant candlesticks, woodruff, primroses, lilies of the valley – each plant had its place. It was a joy to look at.

In front was a row of espaliered pear trees, specially imported from France, and tended so carefully that soon they were bearing as well as they would have done in their homeland.

Where the two old trees had stood was a flagpole flying the Danish flag, and a second pole twined with sweet-smelling hops. In the winter, a sheaf of oats was hung from this pole for the birds to eat at Christmastide; it was an old custom.

"The good Larsen is getting sentimental in his old age," said the master. "But he's a loyal old stick."

In the New Year, one of the illustrated papers carried a picture of the manor house, with the flagstaff and the sheaf of oats. It singled out the sheaf of oats, saying how refreshing it was to see the old traditions kept up in this way.

"Whatever Larsen does gets a fanfare," said the master. "He's a lucky man. We ought to be almost proud to have him."

But they weren't proud. They knew that they were the master and mistress, and they could turn Larsen off with a month's notice if they chose to. They didn't, because they were decent people. There are many like them, which is just as well for the Larsens of this world.

That's the story of "The Gardener and His Master." Make of it what you will.

FATHER'S
ALWAYS RIGHT

NOW I want to tell you a story I heard when I was a boy. It seems to have got better every time I've thought of it since. Stories are like many people – they improve with age, and that's a good thing.

Now you know what a real old farmhouse looks like, with a thatched roof all overgrown with moss and weeds, and a stork's nest on the ridge. The walls are all crooked, and the windows are tiny, and only one of them will open. The bread oven bulges out of the wall like a plump stomach; there's an elderberry hedge, and a little duckpond by the willow tree, with a duck and ducklings on it. In the yard there's an old dog on a chain who barks at anyone who goes by.

Well in just such a farmhouse, out in the country, there lived a farmer and his wife. They had little to spare, but one luxury they had was a horse, which they put out to graze by the side of the road. The farmer would ride it in to town every now and then, or lend it out to friends – and, of course, one good turn deserves another; but all in all, he felt it would be better to sell the horse, or trade it for something more useful. What that would be, he couldn't think.

"You'll know when you see it, Father," said his wife. "It's market day in town today. Why don't you ride in, and sell the horse or exchange it for something. Whatever you do will be right."

She tied on his necktie – she was better at that than he was – and fastened it in a double bow; he did look spruce. She brushed his hat with the palm of her hand, and gave him a kiss, and off he rode on the horse, to sell it or exchange it. Father knew what was what.

It was a sunny day without a cloud in the sky. The road was hot and dusty, and full of people going to market: some driving carts, some riding horses, and some walking on their own two legs. It really was a scorching day, and there wasn't a scrap of shade on the road.

The farmer noticed a man driving a cow along the road – a very fine cow, too. "I bet that cow gives lovely milk," he said to himself. Then he called out, "Hey! You with the cow! Can I have a word?" The man stopped, and the farmer continued, "I suppose a horse is really worth more than a cow, but a cow is more use to me. Will you swap?"

"You bet!" said the man.

And that should be that. The farmer had done the deal, and he should have just turned round and gone home. But he'd been looking forward to the market, and didn't want to miss it. So on he went with the cow.

He strode along, and soon he caught up with a man who was driving a sheep. It was a nice fat sheep, with a woolly coat.

"I like the look of that sheep," thought the farmer. "There's plenty of grazing by the side of the road for a sheep, and in winter it could come into the house. Really, a sheep would be better than a cow." So he called out, "Will you swap?" And of course the man with the sheep was very ready to do so.

The farmer went on with the sheep, until he came to a stile, where he met a man with an enormous goose under his arm. "That's a plump one you've got there," said the farmer. "There's plenty of flesh on that. It would look just right on our pond, and it would be something for Mother to give the vegetable peelings to. She's often said how she'd like a goose – and now she shall have one. Will you swap? I'll give you this sheep for your goose, and throw a thank you into the bargain." The man didn't mind if he did, so they swapped, and the farmer got the goose.

As he came nearer to town, the road grew more and more crowded with animals and folk. They spilled right off the road onto the gatekeeper's potato patch, where he had tethered his hen so that she wouldn't get frightened and stray off. She was a smart short-tailed hen, and she winked her eye at the farmer and said, *"Cluck! Cluck!"* What she meant by it I don't know. The farmer thought, "My, that's a handsome hen, finer than the parson's best. I wish it were mine. A hen can always scratch for its own corn; they don't need much looking after." And he called out, "How about swapping your hen for my goose?" And the gatekeeper thought that was a very good idea, so they did.

The farmer had had a busy morning, and it was a hot day, so he was done in. He could do with a drink and a bite. So he went to the inn. Just as he was going in, he met a servant coming out, carrying a bulging sack.

"What have you got in there?" asked the farmer.

"Rotten apples," said the servant. "I'm taking them to the pigs."

"A whole sackful! I wish Mother could see them. Last year we only got one apple off the old tree by the woodshed; so of course we kept it for a special occasion, and it lay on the chest of drawers until it rotted away. 'It makes me feel quite rich,' Mother used to say. Just think what she'd say to a whole sackful."

"What will you give me for it?" asked the servant.

"This hen," said the farmer. So they swapped.

The farmer made his way into the bar, and leaned his sack of apples up against the potbellied stove, without noticing that it was lit. There were a lot of strangers in the bar – horse-traders, cattle-dealers, even a couple of Englishmen, who were so rich that their pockets were bursting with gold coins. And being English, they would bet on anything.

"*S-s-s! S-s-s!*" What was that noise? It was the apples baking in their skins.

"Whose apples are these?" asked one of the Englishmen.

"Mine," said the farmer, and he told the Englishmen the whole story of how he traded his horse for a cow, and right on down to the sack of rotten apples.

"You'll catch it hot from your wife when you get back," said the Englishmen. "She'll fly off the handle."

"No she won't. She'll give me a kiss, and say, 'Father's always right!'"

 211

"What do you bet?" they asked. "We'll give you a hundred gold coins against whatever you stake."

"I've only got this sack of rotten apples," said the farmer, "but if I lose, you can have Mother and me too. You can't say fairer than that."

"Done!" they said

So the innkeeper fetched his cart, and the Englishmen and the farmer got in, with the rotten apples, and they went to the farmer's house.

"Evening, Mother."

"Evening, Father."

"I've done the deal."

"And got the best of it, I'm sure." The farmer's wife didn't mind the strangers, she went up and gave her husband a big hug.

"I swapped the horse for a cow."

"Thank goodness for the milk," she said. "Now we can make butter and cheese. What a good bargain."

"Then I swapped the cow for a sheep."

"Better still," she replied. "How clever of you. We've got just enough grazing for a sheep, and ewe's milk makes good cheese, and I can spin the wool into yarn and knit woollen socks and nightshirts – cow's hair wouldn't have been any good at all. You think of everything."

"Then I swapped the sheep for a goose."

"Oh Father, you dear man. Are we really going to have goose for the Martinmas feast? You're forever thinking of ways to please me. We can tether the goose and fatten it up for Martinmas."

"Then I swapped the goose for a hen."

"A hen! What a good exchange. Hens lay eggs, and eggs turn into

chicks. I've always wanted to keep hens."

"Then I swapped the hen for a sackful of rotten apples."

"Now I really must give you a kiss; you dear heart! Now listen to me. While you were gone, I thought I must make you a special meal to come home to. I wanted to make you an omelet with chives. I had the eggs, but no chives. So I went to the schoolmaster's; I know they grow chives. But when I asked to borrow some, his wife – the stingy old biddy – just snipped, 'Borrow! Out of the question! Nothing grows in our garden. I couldn't lend you so much as rotten apple.' And now I can lend her ten – a whole sackful, if she wants them! What a hoot, Father!" And she kissed him smack on the lips.

"That's the spirit," said the Englishmen. "Always downhill, but never downhearted. That was worth the money!" And they counted out a hundred gold coins to the farmer whose wife greeted him with kisses not blows.

Yes, it always pays for a wife to think that whatever Father does is for the best.

That's my story. I heard it when I was a boy; and now you have heard it, too, you know that Father's always right.

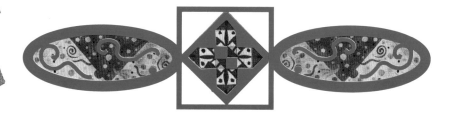

THE SNOWMAN

"It's so cold I'm creaking with it," said the snowman. "It's lovely. The sting in this wind really lets you know you're alive. As for that shiner who thinks she's so bright" – he meant the sun – "she won't outface me. I've got all my bits and pieces under control." For he had two three-cornered bits of tile for eyes, and an old rake for a mouth, with teeth too.

He had been born to the sound of boys' laughter, the jingle of sleigh bells, and the cracking of whips.

The sun set and the moon rose, round and full, clear and calm in the blue night sky. "Here she comes again, from the other direction," said the snowman, who thought it was the sun coming back. "At least I've taught her not to stare so I don't mind if she wants to stay there and light me up. If only I could get the hang of this moving, I'd be well set. First thing I'd do is go and slide on the ice, like the boys do. But I don't know how to run."

"*Gr-off-off!*" barked the old watchdog on his chain. He'd got a sore throat; he'd had it ever since he was pushed out of doors, away from the warm stove. "The sun will teach you how to run. I saw what happened to last year's snowman, and the one before that. Before I can say '*gr-off-off*,' you'll be gone."

"What do you mean, friend?" asked the snowman. "How can that so-and-so up there teach me how to run? I made her run fast enough when I returned her stare, though now she is trying to sneak back the other way."

"You don't know anything," said the watchdog, "but then, they've only just put you up. That one is the moon; the one that went away is the sun. She'll be back tomorrow, and she'll show you how to run all right – all the way to the pond! This weather won't last – I can feel it in my back legs; a change is on the way."

"I don't know what he's getting at," said the snowman, "but I've got an inkling it's not very nice. That one who stared at me and then went away – he called her the sun – is no friend of mine, that's for sure."

"*Gr-off-off!*" barked the watchdog; he turned himself round three times, and lay down in the kennel to sleep.

The weather did change. By morning, the whole landscape was smothered in a thick, clammy fog. Then an icy wind got up, and the frost bit hard. But what a sight it was when the sun came out! The trees and bushes were covered with hoar-frost, like a forest of white coral; every branch was covered with glittering blossom. In summer, the leaves hide the tracery of branch and twig, but now you could see it clearly, like delicate lace, radiant with whiteness. The birch tree swayed in the wind, as full of life as a tree in summer. It was so lovely. And when the sun shone down everything glinted as if it were covered with diamond dust – and the snow itself sparkled like a carpet of diamonds, or thousands of tiny candles, burning whiter than white.

"Isn't it just beautiful?" said a young girl, who was walking in the garden with a young man. "Even lovelier than in summer." And her eyes, too, sparkled.

"And you'd never meet a fellow like this in summer," said the young man pointing to the snowman. "He's splendid."

The girl laughed, and nodded to the snowman; then she and the young man danced back across the snow, which crunched beneath their feet as if they were walking on starch.

"Who were those two?" the snowman asked the watchdog. "'You've been here longer than I have; do you know them?"

"Of course I do," said the watchdog. "She's patted me, oh, many's the time, and he's given me bones; I wouldn't bite *them*."

"But what are they doing here?" asked the snowman.

"Ccc-courting!" said the watchdog. "Soon they'll be moving into a kennel of their own, and gnawing bones together. *Gr-off-off!*"

"And are those two as important as you and I?" asked the snowman.

"Well, they're part of the family," replied the watchdog. "You were only born yesterday, so can't be expected to know these things; I've got the knowledge of experience, I have; I know what's what on this farm. I wasn't always chained up here in the cold. *Gr-off-off!*"

"There's nothing wrong with the cold," said the snowman. "I love it. But tell me more – only please stop rattling your chain, it makes me feel queasy."

"*Gr-off-off!*" barked the watchdog. "I was a puppy once. Oh! Isn't he sweet!' they used to say. I slept indoors on a velvet chair, or even curled up on the mistress's lap. She kissed me on the nose, and wiped my paws with an embroidered handkerchief, and called me 'diddums' and 'dear little puppy-wuppy'. But then I got too big for that, and they gave me to the housekeeper, and I went to live in the basement. You can see right into the very room from where you're standing: that was my domain. It wasn't so fine and luxurious as upstairs, but it was more comfortable. The housekeeper gave me just as good food, and more of it; and I wasn't being constantly petted, or chased by the children. I had my own cushion, and then there was a stove. There's nothing like a stove at this time of the year. I used to crawl right underneath it. Oh, I still dream about that stove. *Gr-off-off! Gr-off-off!*"

"Is a stove nice to look at?" asked the snowman. "Does it look like me?"

"It's exactly the opposite of you. It's coal-black, with a long neck and a brass collar. It eats logs, and breathes flame. Until you've lain

near it – or better still right underneath it – you've no idea what true comfort is. I'm sure you can see it through the window from where you are."

And the snowman looked, and sure enough he saw a shiny black thing with a brass collar, and the gleam of fire. The snowman felt a strange feeling that he couldn't understand – he was thrown off balance in a way all people are sometimes, unless they're made of ice.

"Why did you leave her?" he asked – for he was sure that the stove must be a girl. "How could you bear to?"

"I had no choice," said the watchdog. "They turned me out of doors, and chained me up here, and all because I bit the youngest son in the leg. He took the bone I was gnawing – so, 'a bone for a bone,' thought I. But they didn't see it my way, and from that day I've been chained up, and that was that. It's ruined my voice. *Gr-off-off!* You can hear how hoarse I am."

The snowman had stopped listening. He was gazing into the housekeeper's room in the basement, where the stove stood on its four iron legs; it looked much the same size as the snowman himself.

"I can feel a strange creaking inside," he said. "Shall I ever get into that room? It's an innocent wish, and innocent wishes must surely come true. It's all I wish for, and I wish it with all my heart; so it would be very unfair if it weren't granted. I must get in, and lie beside her, even if I have to break the window."

"You'll never get in," said the watchdog. "And if you did you'd soon go off, *gr-off-off!*"

"I'm as good as off," said the snowman. "I feel I'm breaking apart."

All day long the snowman stared through the window. In the evening, the room looked even more inviting. The stove shone with a soft, warm light that neither the sun nor the moon can make – only a stove. Every time the stove door was opened to feed it, flames leaped out; the snowman's white face blushed red, and the blush went right down to his chest.

"It's more than I can bear," he said. "How beautiful she is when she puts out her tongue!"

The night was long, but not for the snowman. He was happy thinking his own beautiful thoughts, and freezing until he crackled.

In the morning the basement windows were frozen over, frosted with the loveliest ice-flowers any snowman could wish for – but they hid the stove. The ice on the panes just wouldn't thaw, so he couldn't see her. Everything crackled and crunched, it was perfect weather for a snowman, but he couldn't enjoy it. He should have been happy, but he wasn't. He was love-sick for the stove.

"That's a serious problem for a snowman," said the watchdog. "I've suffered that way myself, but I got over it. *Gr-off-off!* The weather's on the change."

And the weather did change. There was a thaw. And the more the weather thawed, the more the snowman thawed. He didn't say anything – not a word – and that's a sure sign.

One morning he collapsed. Where he had been, there was something sticking up, like the handle of a broom; that's what the boys had built him round.

"Now I understand his love-sickness," said the watchdog. "The snowman had a stove rake in his body; that's what set him off. Well, now he's over it. *Gr-off-off!*"

And soon winter was over with too.

"*Gr-off-off!*" barked the watchdog, and the little girls on the farm sang:

> *Now the flowers shall shoot and sprout;*
> *Willow, hang your mittens out.*
> *Lark and cuckoo, soar and sing.*
> *And help us welcome in the spring.*

And no one gave a thought to the snowman.